Tiferet

FOSTERING PEACE THROUGH LITERATURE & ART

ISSN: 1547-2906
ISBN: 9781723993275

Tiferet

AUTUMN/WINTER 2018

FOUNDER & PUBLISHER
Donna Baier Stein

EDITOR-IN-CHIEF
Gayle Brandeis

MANAGING EDITOR
Lisa Sawyer

POETRY EDITOR
Adele Kenny

SUBMISSIONS EDITOR
Jeremy Birkline

ASSISTANT EDITORS
Kristen Turner
Mary Garhart
Pamela Walker

CONTRIBUTING EDITORS
Nancy Lubarsky
Priscilla Orr
Bob Rosenbloom

DESIGNERS & ILLUSTRATORS
Donna Schmitt
Monica Gurevich-Importico

INTERNS
Courtney Harler
Rebecca Kuder
Tate James
Aaron Schwartz
Kate Halse
Kelly Hobkirk
Anne Hoffnagle
Matt Green
Natalie Hirt
Teri Fuller Rouse

COVER ART
"Crane and Sunset" by Hedy Habra

Tiferet

FOSTERING PEACE THROUGH LITERATURE & ART

TIFERET CAN...

Inspire you to write

Connect you to a global community

Lead toward peace in you and in the world

SUBSCRIBE TODAY to enjoy beautiful, inspiring poetry, fiction, creative nonfiction, interviews and visual art from some of today's best writers.

PAST CONTRIBUTORS INCLUDE:

ROBERT BLY   JEAN HOUSTON   ROBERT PINSKY
RAY BRADBURY   STEPHEN DUNN   ED HIRSCH
ILAN STAVANS   ALICIA OSTRIKER   JANE HIRSHFIELD

and so many more . . . Pulitzer Prize winners to newcomers!

You are welcome to submit your own work (*poems, stories, essays, interviews and visual art*) for us to consider for publication. We also run an annual Writing Contest and award $1500 in prizes.
More details can be found at www.tiferetjournal.com.

Tiferet: Fostering Peace though Literature & Art is published twice a year in print and digital formats. We read only electronic submissions made through our website submission feature; submissions made through email attachments or by postal delivery will not be considered.

SUBSCRIPTION INFORMATION: Receive two large volumes per year in your choice of print or digital format.

One Year Subscription $24.95/two or $18.95/two digital
Two Year Subscription $39.95/four print or $35.95/four digital
Three Year Subscription $59.95 /six print or $54.95/six digital
Single Print Issue $14.95 + $3.15 S&H

U.S. currency (cash or check) and Visa, Mastercard, American Express are accepted. For international delivery, extra charges will apply. Please inquire.

ALL OTHER CORRESPONDENCE MAY BE DIRECTED TO:

Tiferet Journal
211 Dryden Road
Bernardsville, NJ 07924

editors@tiferetjournal.com
www.tiferetjournal.com

ISSN 1547-2906 © 2018 AUTUMN/WINTER 2018

Contents

• • • •

"Thank you for this journal which combines spiritual issues, imaginative issues, esthetic issues. All of those, I think, need to be in the mix for the richly lived life, the richly observed life."

– MOLLY PEACOCK, *former President of the Poetry Society of America*

From our Editor-In-Chief

Dearest Readers,

This is a bittersweet letter to write, a letter that marks my final issue of Tiferet as Editor in Chief. While I have chosen to step down from the top of masthead, I remain passionately committed to Tiferet—its mission, its people, the gorgeous, moving, meaningful work it ushers forth, and am excited to witness its evolution from here forward.

This is such a beautiful, heart-filled issue (literally—the word "heart" appears over three dozen times in these pages; appropriate, since one of the meanings of the word Tiferet is "heart") and I am thrilled to be sharing it with you now. In her essay "Zoltar," Phyllis Barber writes "Maybe we have all wished for our wishes to be granted, for fairy godmothers, or for someone, somebody, to listen to our wishes both spoken and not. We want this someone to know our heart's yearnings, to know all the answers, to be wise beyond wisdom and see through walls of granite and steel." While Tiferet is not Zoltar the fortune teller, I wouldn't be surprised if your own heart's yearnings feel seen and heard and known as you read these pages.

We have two special sections in this issue: poems by students and instructors from the Women's Poetry Workshop I was lucky enough to co-teach in Malawi earlier this year and the winners of the Carriage House Poetry Prize—both sections filled with great wisdom and power. I am excited to report that since I wrote my intro to the section of Malawian poetry, Grace Athauye Sharra informed me she received second place in an Africa-wide poetry competition, the only woman on the continent to place. May the voices of Malawian women continue to blast forth into the world.

 "(Poetry) is a magical art and always has been," writes Roger Housden In "Why Poetry for Difficult Times," an excerpt from his book Ten Poems for Difficult Times, "a making of language spells designed to open our eyes, open our doors,and welcome us into a bigger world, one of possibilities we may never have dreamed of…I know that when I meet my own life in a great poem, I feel opened, clarified, confirmed, somehow, in what I always sensed was true but had no words for. Anything that can do this is surely necessary for the fullness of a human life." Every piece in this journal—poetry and prose—has this power, the power to open, to clarify, to confirm.

"Everything we have we're given/in love to use in love, in grace./There is nothing we alone have written," writes Susan Rogers in her poem, "Grateful Conversations"; this makes me think of the collaborative nature of a magazine, as well. I am so deeply grateful for the conversations I've had through Tiferet—conversations with the writers in our pages, conversations with our wonderful staff, conversations with dear Donna Baier Stein, the visionary founder and publisher of this beautiful journal. I look forward to continuing these conversations from a different bench. All of it given in love, to use in love.

With all my heart, all my gratitude,
Gayle Brandeis

POETRY

The Heart Is a Muscular Organ

Melissa Studdard

Each morning when I wake I pray
to be a channel of divine blessings to all I encounter.
By noon I'm pissed off at someone
and like a chopper full of soldiers I carry god inside me.
They're dressed in camo and boots
haven't bathed in a week
can't quite remember how they got there.
By dusk I've bathed god a hundred times in the hidden
light of compassion
changed them out of camo into cool pastels
unlaced the fighter boots and restrapped the sandals.
My heart then is like a little forest clearing with the one
patch of sun shining all on god and the people who piss me off.
The truth is sometimes I get tired of being human
and I walk through the darkest part of my aorta
collecting tiny flowers that grow hidden under rocks and leaves
the size of giants' feet.
This is how I learn to pray.
O God, I say, let me be devoured by a pack of lions.
O Lord, please let me be reborn as mane.

NONFICTION

Are We Lost in the Wilderness?

Susan J. Tweit

Here in Wyoming, Lent, when Christians commemorate the time Jesus spent in the wilderness, blew in on a blizzard. Only five hardy souls made it to the eight o'clock service at my neighborhood church in Cody.

As drifts piled up outside and the temperature plummeted, our rector, Reverend Mary Caucutt, reminded us that the word "wilderness" encompasses opposing meanings: it can be a place of solace and retreat, of spiritual and emotional cleansing. It can also mean a place of danger and anxiety, of trial and tribulation.

It feels like we, the American people, are stumbling in some moral wilderness of the second sort, numb to the exploits of a president who routinely bullies those he disagrees with, boasts about abusing women, and glibly spreads chaos and lies. Numb to the gutting of our social safety nets, environmental laws, public land protections, and voting rights. Numb, in fact, to the erosion of the very qualities that make us human.

If these times are a test of our humanity, it seems to me that we are close to failing.

As we stumble through this dark time, it is apt to remember that wilderness offers both challenge and opportunity: it is that thicket of fears and doubts which snares us and causes us to stumble into despair, and also the journey that offers clarity and enlightenment. As a literal landscape, wilderness encompasses that duality as well: it is the wild unknown we fear, as well as the unspoiled refuge we mythologize and long for.

Like many westerners, I prize wilderness. I have fled to the challenging sanctum of the wild at times when I desperately needed discernment and healing, needed to hear the "small, still voice" of my better self amid the babel of chaotic times.

Twice, I backpacked solo across the Greater Yellowstone Ecosystem, carrying all I needed on my back as I trekked through some of the wildest country in the lower forty-eight. Those days and miles of walking alone, talking to myself as I navigated country that belongs more to the resident grizzly bears and wolves than to we humans, reminded me forcefully that I am small. That my life is one track among many, and that some would not hesitate to eat me for lunch. Feeling that, eyes and ears attuned to danger, clarifies what matters.

In the wilderness, I could not escape myself—either the parts I celebrate or the parts I prefer to hide. I had to rely on who I really am, not who I'd prefer to be. Wilderness time taught me how precious and precarious this life we often take for granted is: one misstep and we may disappear for good, our flesh becoming food for ravens and coyotes, our bones gnawed by hungry mice.

That blizzardy Sunday in Cody, Reverend Mary pointed out that Lent is a time of searching, a time to act on the lessons we have learned from our experiences in real or metaphorical wilderness.

If we and our society are to make it out of this moral wilderness of our own creation, we must reclaim our shared humanity. Step up and grow up, and be the best of our species.

Which, to me, means acting from love and compassion and respecting our differences. Summoning the courage to speak truth to power, to say that global climate change and the extinction of species and cultures is morally wrong. That owning automatic weapons is not a constitutional right. That using power to demean or exploit others is always wrong, no matter who you are.

That we are stronger and our communities are healthier when we work together. When we all rise. When we nurture the web of life that makes this planet home to us all.

Perhaps we needed to be lost in order to see where we went wrong, to find the courage and strength to stand up for what is right in our county and our lives, and to fix what is not. Perhaps we are on our way to learning how to be more fully and beautifully human.

POETRY

Without Longing, How to Make Beautiful the Song?

Marie-Elizabeth Mali

Anywhere you drop the needle on my heart's record
it lands on absence, a song with longing for a hook
and a groove so irresistible I repeat it on every track:
husband who traveled for a living, divorce, new lover
in a country so far away he lived in tomorrow.

*

Even the longing is lovely—a line in an old poem
about a once-sparkled heart darkened by forgetting.

*

The chocolate ganache on the white plate I stare at,
salivating, is nine-times-out-of-ten more delicious
than the ganache I put in my mouth.

This is also true of most men.

*

Back when I used to sing jazz, my best numbers
were torch songs, the unrequited heart thrown
on the stage and left to bleed in the spotlight.

*

When I led kirtan, by the second or third chant, a shift—
the song no longer a heart locked in a basement
crying to something untouchable, but a call and response

Tiferet

from sky to itself. But I never started the kirtan there
and would return—in a way, with relief—
to longing's familiar quarters after the final *om*.

*

The nearby male humpback whale's song thrums
my body human into harp strings, so filled with longing
for a mate he hangs nose-down and sings a cycle of grunts,
whistles, and slide notes to broadcast his desire.

*

There's no pride in longing. After a breakup I traveled
to dive in the country where he was born. I looked
for him in faces, heard him in every local figure of speech,
wanted to lick each grain of sand on a beach
he'd once walked in case it had touched his feet.

NONFICTION

Zoltar

Phyllis Barber

In the 1988 movie, "Big," Tom Hanks plays the wished-big side of a puny seventh grader by the name of Josh—a skinny, underdeveloped kid. Tired of being a shrimp and ignored by the tall girl of his dreams, Josh takes his fervent wish to be "big" to the end of a deserted alley at the dark edge of a carnival in town for a one-night stand. There, Zoltar sits inside a lighted booth, encased within glass walls. Waiting. Mysterious. An inescapable, beckoning finger.

Zoltar, of the sharp nose and beady eyes that light up when a fortune is about to be divulged. Zoltar, the gypsy with the marionette mouth. The fortune teller who wears a red and purple turban wound together and pinned by a vast ruby, a high beaded collar, and a jeweled necklace laid flat over the shoulders of his brocaded robe. This is an exotic necromancer/wizard from the land of magic lanterns and people disappearing behind scarves and veils. He maintains a larger presence than most wax or papier mâché figures. And it is here, pleading to Zoltar, that Josh, played by David Moscow, finds his most magical fortune delivered in an ordinary slot: "Your wish is granted." And the next morning, the young boy awakes as a "big" Josh, a big Tom Hanks.

Your wish is granted.

Magic words.

Maybe we have all wished for our wishes to be granted, for fairy godmothers, or for someone, somebody, to listen to our wishes both spoken and not. We want this someone to know our heart's yearnings, to know all the answers, to be wise beyond wisdom and see through walls of granite and steel. Maybe that's why Tom Hanks' man-kidness/coltness was appealing as well as heartbreaking. He wanted to be Bigger than Big. A man. I wanted him to be Big, too. I wanted him to have his wishes granted, no doubt about it. I knew a little bit of what he'd been feeling. After all, I'd been a 5'9" beanpole in the seventh grade with too long of arms and legs to tuck in a tidy package.

But Josh was a kid, bottom line. Somewhere in the maze of my mind, there was this nagging thought. What would it mean to have a boy's wish granted? What price had to be paid to receive that wish? What did karma have in store for someone who opposed the natural order and disrupted the passage of life?

Tiferet

The film's writer must have had that bothersome thought as well, as Hanks ends up not being very happy in his "man" state. He longs to be a kid again, even if an awkward one. He's a kid at heart. He's tired of being a big person with serious responsibilities. And luckily, he's able to return to the boy he once was. Nice to have the film end in innocence before Josh's voice changes and oily pimples come fast and furious.

* * * * *

When I was visiting Las Vegas years later, the Venetian to be exact, walking in the Grand Canal while a gondolier sang to a couple holding hands in his boat ("O Solo Mio"), a place where one is not surprised to see a monkey on a chain hooked to an organ grinder endlessly turning the crank on his hurdy gurdy, I was suddenly facing Zoltar myself. The same Zoltar. The one I'd seen in the movie.

The sight of the magician in a glass case was no small moment. Like he was there for a reason. His eyes shifted just enough to let me know he was for real and that he'd been waiting for me all these many years.

"Zoltar," I said in a lightning-bolt voice. My young female companion looked at me as if I were beyond daft. She had no reason to recognize this genie-in-a-box.

"Who's Zoltar?" she asked, and I wanted to put an elbow in her eye.

"Who's Zoltar!" I said, in a voice full of awe at her lack of intelligence. "You don't know Zoltar?"

I reached in my pocket. I fumbled for money that would give me passage to Zoltar's world, where I could hear his voice speaking from the Land of Insistent and Unbelievable Magic, all the time a carousel-type calliope playing whole tone scales creating an exotic desert music. I put a quarter in the slot beneath the 25 cent sign, though the engraving was worn, and held my breath. I listened to the money clank into the innards of Zoltar's world.

And then he spoke. In a commanding voice. My shoes were riveted to the floor. Stuck to the concrete. Me in front of The Great Zoltar! Hearing him speak. To me!

"You will see much that you never anticipated seeing. You will travel far and wide."

And then, all too soon, he stopped. Cold. His mouth settled into its former straight line. His features had no expression.

All of that for those few words? For 25 cents?

But he remained silent.

I was disappointed. The fortune had been so common, and much too brief for my expectations. I wanted to say, "Tell me more, Zoltar, Fount of All Wisdom. Don't be silent." No more words from Zoltar came, however, and I became aware of the what-I-now-considered-as normal sounds of the Grand Canal around me and the absence of my companion. That's all he had to say?

But then I saw a yellow ticket sliding out from a metal slot at the base of the glass case. Yes, there was more. There were further words from Zoltar. Further insights into his deep-desert-night wisdom touched with the scent of Araby. I grabbed the card-stock ticket, needing to read something I should have known all of these years. I rubbed my thumb over the barely-raised printing. And I looked up at Zoltar just to make sure he had nothing more to say. He just stared. His only job was to wait for coins to roll into the coin slot. That was the only way he could be bothered with the revelation of more deep, dark secrets.

At least I had a souvenir in my hand. I turned it over. Anticipating. And I read, "I see a great deal of happiness in store for you. You will receive a letter soon, and that letter can easily be said to change the whole course of your life."

The whole course of my life? That's a big change at my age. I don't have a lot of course left. Do I want a letter that can change that now? What would it have to say to cause such a seismic occurrence? Fame? Lots of money? And what would I do with mega-money at this point, except give it away to family and charity? Though all of these can use financial support, I grant you. Or would the letter tell me that my writing has finally been recognized beyond my wildest dreams: "You have just been nominated for the Nobel Prize in Literature," or maybe, "Your book is the number one choice in the NY Times Centennial Favorites List?" But those are my first thoughts, those paltry thoughts of fame and fortune which I should have given up a while back. I'm more mature than that. Having the public go ga-ga over you for any reason is overrated. All those paparazzi. The crowds tearing at your clothes. Zoltar must know that by now.

But what about mail that says, "Your husband and his Parkinson's are in for a big surprise. We have found a simple cure, an inexpensive and thorough cure?" What about a letter that says, "Your sons' musical talent has been discovered and five record labels are pursuing them and five movie producers want them to write scores for their latest films? They will never have to look for an agent, producer, or audience again. The world knows their worth."

But would that change the whole course of MY life? What about my own life? What would matter to me, just me?

But then, I can't help myself. I'm thinking—a nasty habit of mine. Don't my husband and children's lives impact my own? A life can't be lived alone, I argue internally. Impossible. Mothers, fathers, sisters, brothers, children, friends, teachers can be our happiness, maybe even our sorrow, but they're a part of who we are, of what we've become. A reward just for one person, for just me, seems a strange thing when you think about it. None of us got here by ourselves, no way, so that is an interesting question: what would be the news that would change the course of one's whole life and bring happiness? Not your friends', children's, loves' or neighbors' lives, but your own?

I read on. "You deserve this happiness because you have been so faithful and sincere in your love."

And at that moment, everything changed. The scrim dropped. "Zoltar!" I said out loud, feeling like a scolding school teacher at the head of a class. "You've stooped to using positive reinforcement with your fortune-telling?"

I didn't need rewards with my fortunes. I could see around those corners! Who really deserves anything anyway? And why do I deserve more than the next person? Everyone works hard, though some work at things that bring in rewards to a greater degree, I'll grant you that. But why do I deserve happiness because I've been faithful and sincere in my love? Shouldn't I just love? And "sincerely" means real love anyway, doesn't it? On top of that, if I just loved myself, I'd be a pretty lonely cookie. Nobody to talk to. Monologue. Interior dialogue. Enough of that already. So my happiness isn't just a matter of me, myself, and I, but of all the others who talk, laugh, kibbutz, joke, tease, tell stories, rib, cajole, teach, instruct, inform me every day in every way.

"However, if you wish to continue to be happy," the fortune continued, "you'll have to learn not to be too trustworthy. Avoid the flatterers and be a little more careful in choosing your friends."

Zoltar, now you're lecturing. Your magic isn't simple but rather prescriptive.

But, then I settle from my outrage. Maybe I'm the one to blame for expecting something simple or profound or impossible from your fortunes. I can't help myself. It's the nature of the beast. But how can I keep my mind from thinking about Zoltar's words? From turning them over and mulling the angle of the point? I counted on the magician. I did. I believed in him, even if that may seem silly, maybe because Tom Hanks believed in him, or at least the boy Josh did.

But life isn't a matter of magic, I conclude as I turn to find my companion who has wandered off to window shop, ready to waltz along the Grand Canal once again. I want to believe. I so want to believe in magic wands and fairy godmothers and Zoltars. Wouldn't that be quite a world, where things hopped that usually walked, where horses flew through air, where toads walked upright and with a cane. Maybe I'm too suspicious of magic prevailing against the order of things. Maybe I believe that'll never happen. Maybe I'm a sludge. A pounder. A one foot in front-of-the-other kind of person and not in too big of a hurry to change the order of the world. But at least I'll try to be grateful for what I have, what I had before I ever met or heard about you, Zoltar.

FICTION

Skies

Tovli Simiryan

Out of a clear blue sky, I remember them. Our grandmother begged us not to forget our beginning, the sound darkness made inside forests or how deep the ocean was the first time we looked beyond its waves. Even in dark places, I have learned where to find light. Every year, the opaque *año* candle is stubborn. Each year, its flame is more difficult to kindle. I tell myself it is taking its time to breathe, reminding the world of obligations. Its plump little soul, good for at least twenty-five hours, looks into my eyes, burns the tips of my fingers and asks, "What did you remember first?"

In my first memory, it is almost morning. My grandfather is teaching. His voice is calm, deliberate, and everyone listens. I smile into his face. "Big Papa, it's cold outside."

He places his finger to his lips and describes the colored stones cemented into soil that will predict our path. I see trees, their heads disappearing like tethered rockets about to launch themselves skyward. Their limbs are heavy. They drop toward the ground and I grab handfuls of green leaves. I think the trees will miss us. I imagine they are begging to follow us.

What was left of our family and village? A young woman's eyes watched her feet instead of her children. Grandma held her frayed head scarf tight beneath her chin, as though the loss of body-heat would never be forgiven. Big Papa, her husband, was strong, but thin. He was our leader. He advised and demanded, "No talking. Stay quiet. Keep them quiet. Everyone, stay on the path."

Each year, the flickering flame of the memorial candle demands I recall this first memory, an endless path with whole pieces of stone forced into the earth pointing toward one destiny. We walked it. The path, I mean. It was uneven, built from shrewd effort and full of surprises. There were cracks and pieces of gravel erupting from its soul. Grandma fell. Big Papa whispered to his wife, "Careful, careful." The soft faces of babies leaned over their parent's shoulders and looked down at us.

The forest had rooms, like a castle. It loomed in darkness on both sides of our footsteps. The stone path presupposed our safety. The dark trees wiggled their

giant toes from beneath the ground and tickled the stones until the cement buckled as though laughing. My brother and I smiled into the faces of the babies, their cheeks turning red from an icy wind, their parents focused, perturbed with our love of adventure and desire to bolt into the darkness and close the doors behind us. *Children. This is not a game.* Who said it? I have forgotten.

I recall the forest more clearly than the path of frightened people moving toward something foreign, something unseen, yet planned. Even in darkness, the forest was green. By day, its colors changed. The sky joined the dense leaves the way Grandma fit rags together, sewing pieces into a comfortable quilt that kept us warm and proud. The blue air became a breeze, the leaves moved, showing silver under-bellies, predicting rain that never touched the ground, shedding what no longer mattered and covering the land with brown, crisp carpeting.

We played there, making castles that blew away, crying to our grandfather: *Big Papa, Big Papa, our castle is gone.* We learned what fell to the wind amidst our forest was never lost. Forests themselves are fortresses with a myriad of rooms to play and hide in, and some rooms should never be opened.

At night, the trees were one color. If you looked far into the forest's core, even while walking along the stone path—with worried parents leading our way, cloth sacks filled with food unlikely to spoil and water jars sloshing inside blankets—the leaves became the night, a cloud of darkened air, moonless with no knowledge of stars. The forest was the enemy at sunset and our sustenance by day.

It was a narrow path. I remember this because Grandma told me: "We'd fall and drop the food sacks. Mothers tripped and fell into the tall weeds that lined the road. The young girl broke her ankle. She had no man. He had been taken the day before. We could not wait for him."

I don't actually remember that part. But thanks to Grandma, I can tell the young girl's story as though it happened to me. She was a thin, petite girl who had her third baby just before the first bomb hit. It was an easy birth. Grandma said the gardens were rich that season. Women planning summer births had the greenest vegetables and orchards yielded prolific amounts of fruit. Everything was unusually sweet that year. Her baby was the first born of the summer months. He was such a good little baby and every woman in the village cried from hope and joyfulness.

When we ran, Big Papa helped her wrap the baby in burlap, tying the bundle in such a way the infant could nurse and the young girl could see his face and not lose hope in the future.

Grandma explained so many times, "She didn't want to leave. She was afraid her husband would not be able to find her when he returned. But we made her run with us."

Tiferet

"Grandma. Why didn't you wait with her — for her husband I mean?"

"He was already dead. Big Papa found him along the road two days before we escaped. They'd caught him. One of the soldiers shot him."

"No one told her?"

"No one told. We were going to tell her later, in a gentle way. You can't run when your shadow has been ripped from your skin. We tried to save her life." Grandma was old when she explained this to me. "Sometimes, Babeleh, memories aren't really memories, but legacy. Memory is often the seam endurance makes when you must choose quickly in the middle of the night to survive."

Sometimes Grandma woke from her naps suddenly, asking, "Did you light the memorial candle this year? Tell, me, what do you remember first?"

I would hold her hand gently, revealing, "I remember the day my shadow became uneven and our faces began changing."

I could not see my shadow for many years following the escape. Sometimes, even now, I worry it's missing. I worry change has left me paralyzed and unrecognizable. When I am in the park just a half mile from our home, tucked sweetly inside the confines of America, my shadow is that of the frail, thin girl who wanted to stay behind. When I look to see if my shadow is still attached, I remember Grandma and her stories. As she aged, her memory of the young, thin mother became as clear and deep as the ocean we'd crossed to recapture belonging.

Grandma's story-voice was like the man-made, rocky path, broken and sharp in places. At times, she fought back tears. Mostly she spoke in pieces as though quilting: stretching the cloth into stories, knowing when to relax her hold just before the material tore. She weaved memory, stitching along at just the right speed and angle until every thread had its place, every color had been returned to where she'd first learned about its existence and demise. Every story was about my first memory—the path out, the ones we left behind, the lost shadows, the frail mother holding her third child, both wounded forever.

"The young girl fell from the stone path. The rocks were jagged and rough. It was just before dawn and there was very little light. We chose the night no moon would be visible. Do you remember the stones, Babeleh?"

"I remember the path, Grandma. I remember your scarf and the red cheeks of the babies."

"Do you remember the petite girl? What happened to her?"

"She fell. First, she fell to her knees and the stones cut her skin to the bone. She fell on the baby. Big Papa cursed under his breath. His breath smelled like a cigar. It made me think we were still home, but we weren't. We were running and hiding, running and hiding.

"The thin girl looked up at the sky and said, 'I think I can see the stars. The moon is about to rise. It looks like a storm. I see lightning.' She was so frail. I remember her eyes. They were dark brown, always watching for blue skies—even at night she believed in blue skies and splendid orchards that bordered fertile gardens.

"Everyone, not just Big Papa, begged her to be quiet, but she cried out. The baby cried too. The sound from their bodies pierced the cold like two sharp arrows with nothing left to aim for. It was as if her pain had become joy and she screamed, 'Oh. Thank God—it's Herschel, my husband. My Herschel is following us. I see him between the leaves and starlight.'

"And there *were* stars, Grandma. There were many stars that sliced the night into pieces and illuminated every stone and every fingernail. The moon rose between the trees of the forest as though it were bringing dawn instead of the stars. I remember this, Grandma. It is the first thing I remember in my life."

"It happened." Grandma grasped the ends of her scarf and held it close to her chin the way she did the night we escaped, as though proving all memory was valid and not merely needed to cover hair that had turned white and was about to disappear forever. "It always happens this way."

"The thin girl was killed. I remember the cheeks of her baby were not burnt red from the cold, but were splashed with the blood of its tiny mother. The baby's face was cut from being dropped against the sharp stones that were supposed to lead us to safety. The baby's blood and its mother's were like one, flowing wound."

"We ran when the shooting started. Some of us were captured. We never saw them again." Grandma dropped sugar cubes into her tea when she confirmed this part of the memory. "They took Jonah."

I remembered my brother, less than a year younger than I, being pulled into the dark air of the forest by hands clad in leather gloves. I could still smell the musk beneath the leaves that swirled from the forest floor as his feet dangled at eye level and Big Papa grabbed my arm, pulling Grandma and me into the trees. There we hid, silent, motionless, fearing the rising sun would reveal what was left of our shadows and the enemy would follow our trail.

Grandma confirmed, always reluctantly: "We lost your brother. We never knew what happened to him. After the war, we hoped he would return from one of the camps. But we never saw him again."

"Was it the thin girl's fault, even though she and the baby were shot?" I always asked this question just before Grandma sipped her tea, careful not to scald her lips and tongue.

"Babeleh, there is never fault, only a seam. The thin girl was lonely. She missed her husband. When women grieve, it is as though they remember before an event has reached completion. It's as if grief makes a woman leave the world as memory instead of principle. A grieving woman is never ready for change."

My first memory is of dawn approaching, colored stone in darkness and splendor that became war ripping our shadows from beneath our feet. Memory is more dangerous than the ones who chased and hated us because our accent differed, our language had opportunity for metaphor, our food took longer to prepare, or our clothes were made from scratch and the thread that held us together could not be weakened by anyone other than our God. Memory seeps from continent to continent, absorbing lost shadow as though apparitions were real people, no longer dead, no longer running for the next border or train. In memory they are healed of wounds, laughing from joy and admiring the density of trees nestled so close together they might as well be grave markers unable to be moved.

Grandma died softly and quickly, like Big Papa. She closed her eyes and remembered my frail mother, her daughter, the tiny girl from the war, looking for Herschel in every crack, pressing the first baby of summer to her breast and watching her feet instead of her other children.

An hour before Grandma's death, we played the memory game. "Babeleh, don't forget to light our memorial candle this year. Tell me, what do you remember first?"

"The same, Grandma: I remember every story and every fear." But this time, I told her, with the quiet voice of an adult, "Grandma, I miss Jonah and our forest. My first memory? I was ashamed Mama cried out, mistaking bullets for stars and bombs for the moon. I wanted to grab Jonah and run from you and Big Papa and hide in the forest. We wanted to close the doors after us and pull our shadows inside our souls so they'd never be lost. Grandma, can you forgive this memory?"

"Always, Babeleh. Memory is shadow looking for its own little story. Sometimes it hides inside rooms that never open."

Her voice ended abruptly. Her eyes darkened with tears as though iris and pupil converged. I looked carefully into what was left; feeling cold, as though the future was really the past, and the time might come when I would stop remembering and no longer exist. It was as if every dead shadow suddenly attached itself to my body falling like one final piece of shrapnel against the floor.

I said, "Grandma, did you hear the sound of shadows falling? It was quite a thud." I opened every window and she flew like lightning into a blue sky.

Heidi Clapp-Temple   ENTWINED LIFE

NONFICTION

Taking Flight

David Yasuda

The hummingbird lies still and cold in my wife Katy's hand. It's about four inches long with bright emerald green feathers and a brilliant fuchsia neck. The colors are so vibrant and iridescent, the diminutive creature does not seem real.

"I've never seen a hummingbird up this close," I say in a quiet voice. I want to reach out and touch it, but I let my eyes do the inspection, afraid I might damage the fragile animal.

"He's beautiful," Katy says. She gently examines him. "His wings and legs are flexible. I think there's a chance he's alive. Maybe he hit a window and is just stunned."

The poor little soul looks very dead to me.

"Does it feel warm?" I ask.

"He's so tiny, I can't tell."

As if on cue, he blinks his eye.

We look at each other in amazement and disbelief.

"Go inside the donut shop and make some sugar water!" Katy orders. She has kicked into life-saving mode and her sense of urgency is set to maximum strength.

Moments earlier, we were walking down Mississippi Avenue in Portland's Northside with Katy's sixteen-year-old son, Fox, enjoying our final hours of a weekend visit. The historical average temperature for February is fifty-one degrees, but unseasonably cold weather arrived and the mercury dropped to thirty-three. Snow fell the night before and we carefully made our way through the icy patches on the walkways toward our destination. Our goal was to beat the morning crowd lined up at Blue Star Donuts. The day before, Katy, Fox, and I had arrived at the door just in time to watch them sell their last order.

Blue Star puts out a truly unique product. They are to donuts what Portland's Salt & Straw is to ice cream, David Chang is to ramen, or In-N-Out is to fast food burgers. Their lovely round pastries are much elevated from the grocery store, deep-fried versions of my childhood. The menu lists unique offerings like blueberry bourbon basil, raspberry rosemary buttermilk, and chocolate almond ganache. I walked at a brisk pace, holding Katy's hand, focused on procuring a donut, maybe two, and a cup of coffee.

Just as the shop was in sight, Fox made a run for the door and Katy stopped. I tugged at her arm like a little kid set on being the first in line to see Santa, but she let go of my hand and pointed to the ground.

"Look!" she called out. Her keen and discerning eyes immediately noticed something out of the ordinary on the sidewalk. I glanced at the ground, but didn't immediately see the cause of her alarm. She knelt down and scooped up the motionless hummingbird.

Now that the injured bird demonstrates signs of life, I follow Katy's directions.

"Make the sugar water in a 4:1 ratio, four parts water to one part sugar," she says, drawing from her experience of making the solution for our hummingbird feeder at home.

I have seen my wife like this before. When we walk around our neighborhood or hike in the local foothills back in Boise, Katy's eyes scan the area for wild things. We were taking an evening stroll along the Boise River and she spotted a salamander that had become stranded on the asphalt walkway. She picked it up and spent twenty minutes trying to find an area that was damp, but not wet, and hidden from excitable children and possible predators. I have also watched and assisted with her rescue of cats, dogs, snakes, frogs, caterpillars, fish and, of course, this one particular hummingbird.

Katy has been an amateur animal rescuer for most of her life. Starting at the age of six or seven, she was attracted to injured birds, rodents and miscellaneous small animals in need of care. She kept her patients in empty shoe boxes lined with rags or paper towels and tried her best to nurse them back to health. Few of her early efforts were successful, but she studied library books about animals and their care. For further education, she watched the Wild Kingdom, documentaries about living things and any animal-related programs she could find. Up until she was in high school, her career path was to be a veterinarian. Like many would-be animal doctors, the rigors of the advanced sciences waylaid her plans, but Katy continued her informal studies and hands-on practices. Today, she teaches high school art, but continues to be a wealth of knowledge of how to treat sick animals and has a high success rate of curing sick or injured critters and releasing them back into the wild.

Tiferet

I run into Blue Star and the rich, sweet aroma of fresh made donuts immediately hits me. I see Fox waving at me expectantly from the pastry case and I'm surprised to find we're the first customers in the store. My immediate reaction is to place an order and Fox's deliberately raised eyebrows tell me he is thinking the same thing. The customer service person is absent at the front counter, but we can hear someone moving boxes in the back of the store.

"I'll be right out!" says a friendly male voice.

My stomach growls at the thought of breakfast, but my attention goes back to the rescue mission. I locate the self-serve water dispenser and follow Katy's directions. I tear a sugar packet open, eye it and approximate what four times the amount of water should be. There is not a stir stick, so I use my finger to mix the solution. As I finish up, Katy walks through the front door with the bird cradled in her hands.

"Good morning!" says the bright-eyed, young man as he emerges from the back of the store. He has wavy, blond hair and sports a pinkish skin tone, as if he has recently emerged from a tanning bed. Even though he wears the Blue Star uniform t-shirt, his look and vibe is much more SoCal than PDX. "What can I get you?"

"We found a hummingbird and he needs a little first aid. Do you have something we can put him in?" asks Katy.

"Well, we have this *donut box*," he says with just a hint of sarcasm and a forced smile. While trying to be considerate, he clearly finds this out of the range of his job requirements and does not appear to be an animal lover. He eyes the bird suspiciously and extends his arm fully so he doesn't accidentally come into contact with it.

I take the box from his hands and look for something soft to pad it with. When I turn around, I see a crowd of patrons have begun to form a line in front of the counter. Fox is standing off to the side, eyeing the Blue Star's specialties beckoning him from behind the glass.

"Hold a place in line for us!" I quietly bark at Fox. "I'll be back in a minute." He knows his mother can't be deterred from her animal care duty, rolls his eyes, and takes a spot at the end of the line. While my appetite for some amazing donuts is not quite as strong as my desire to save the bird, I see no reason we can't have it all.

Katy and I stand by the water station away from the counter, hummingbird in hand, and debate how to get the food to his mouth. There are no straws available, which is very PC and eco-friendly, but not helpful when trying to bring a near-death bird back to life.

"I'm not sure about putting his beak in the solution" says Katy and then decides to try to feed our patient with her fingers. She dips her index finger into the sugar water and rubs it on his beak.

"Is he eating?" I ask.

"I still can't tell."

I can see Fox on the opposite side of the shop. A few more people walk through the front door and take their place behind him. He looks my way and I shrug. Katy continues to dip her finger into the sugar water and put in on the little bird's beak. She looks up for a moment to talk to me and suddenly our friend's wings beat and he tries to fly. Katy quickly closes her hands to contain the bird.

"He's OK!" she says.

"Let's go outside," I say "It would be a disaster if he got loose in here."

The bird remains alert but motionless and we walk outside to find a tree or shrub that is out of the way. Nothing looks promising in our immediate area.

"It looks like there's a park across the street," I say, "let's try over there."

We cross Mississippi Avenue, walk away from the street and find a greenspace between a building and parking lot. A row of small trees lines the side and direct sunshine is slowly warming our surroundings. Katy spies a tree with a branch that can protect our ward from human eyes and potential attackers. As she opens her hand to set the bird on the branch, his head perks up, he flaps his wings and with a distinctive buzzing sound, and our friend the hummingbird flies away. He darts around our heads, then does a straight vertical climb. The brightly colored bird hovers a moment, as if to say "thank you," then moves on.

I look at Katy, she looks at me, and we both laugh out loud.

"That was amazing!" I say.

"Sometimes you get lucky," she answers.

"That bird was lucky you saw him."

Katy nods and reaches for my hand.

I look up, searching for a dot of green. All I see is open sky. He is gone, but the moment is still magical, and we are both giddy from our shared experience.

We walk across the street to rejoin Fox, still in line at Blue Star. When we get to the front, we're still riding the excitement from the hummingbird's rescue and recovery.

"Thanks for your help earlier," Katy says to the blond counter guy. "He perked up and flew away."

"Oh, that's nice" he says, polite but clearly unimpressed. "What can I get you?"

Tiferet

The three of us split two donuts, a poppy seed lemon and a chocolate almond ganache. They're tasty and satisfying, but nothing really compares to breathing life into a seemingly dead creature.

We drive out of Portland on snowy roads, a strange sight here in the usually temperate Pacific Northwest. The customary lush green surroundings are covered in white, giving the morning an enchanted feel. Katy does some research and confirms the bird she saved is an Anna's Hummingbird, named after Anna Masséna, Duchess of Rivoli. Katy reads more facts. Anna's is the only hummingbird that can spend the entire winter this far north. They sometimes supplement their nectar diet with insects. Flowers and bird feeders in suburban gardens have altered their migration habits.

I listen intently and Fox becomes more engrossed in his Nintendo DS. The further east we drive, the more we slip back into our normal rhythm. We'll arrive home in a few hours, unpack the car and get ready for work and school. Our lives are directed by a list of things that keeps our family moving forward. Buy groceries, cook food, do the laundry, sweep the floor, take out the garbage, make the bed. I find a small bit of satisfaction in completing these simple tasks. My work provides its own rewards of projects completed and objectives met, but the surprises received from the natural world are what make us feel alive. The glow of a sunrise, a hot wind blowing in the darkness of the night, the sound of a hummingbird as it moves from blossom to branch. These are the things that create moments of wonder and allow our minds to take flight.

Poems from the Malawian Women's Poetry Workshop

In March, 2018, I had the beautiful opportunity to co-teach a women's poetry workshop at the Jacaranda Cultural Center in Blantyre, Malawi. My fellow teachers, all amazing poets and artists—Mildred Barya, TJ Dema, and Jumoke Sanwo—and I were so moved and inspired by the women who came to the workshop and the poetry they produced, as were Beverley Nambozo Nsengiyunva and Susan Kiguli, who facilitated a separate session. During the workshop, we learned that very few Malawian women writers are known outside their home country. Their voices need to be heard—I am so delighted and honored to provide space for some of our students (as well as some of the instructors) here now. --Gayle Brandeis

Beauty

Xara Hlupekile

Your daughter does not love herself. She, trades her body
for scraps of love struggles with her shade of ebony stays
out of the sun eats a little keep in even less.

Your daughter accepts less than, gives more than
tries to escape her body most nights wakes up with a
knife in her bed silently begs to be loved loudly settles
for Tuesday or Thursday night. Attracts men like you,
loves men like you.

And no this is not because your favorite daughter is the one with the light skin
your favorite child the son you have with a white woman or that you since you met
her you have told her to eat a little exist even less.

POEMS FROM THE MALAWIAN WOMEN'S POETRY WORKSHOP

KWIBUKA
(for genocide victims in Rowanda 1991)

Grace Athauye Sharra

Kwibuka O Daughter of Africa that day sometime in April
When the sun suddenly had to set one morning and man fell
And monstrous Grendel descended smiling, wagging his demonic tail

Kwibuka how the sooted gates of Hell swung open so broad
Spitting legions of dark lean demons that gushed forward
Clinking and clashing machete, coming for your blood

Kwibuka Africa's Own, how they came and dragged you to hell
All those dark angels towering over you, tolling that chilling knell
As Cain's machete whizzed and whistled hacking little Abel

Kwibuka Haunted daughter those gruest, coldest hundred days
That you felt a million death, lost your innocence in all ways
As Cain bathed in Abel's blood, desecrating your motherhood for always

A hundred days Grendel kept you hostage in that dark tower
Nibbling at your flesh as the sun wept blood tears in that hour
As dark clouds shrouded sanity and flaunted the darkest Hell's power

A hundred days you walked through the valley of death
Saw your slain young ones and wrestled many a wraith
Groaned many a ramasabaktan, lost a great deal of hope and faith

A hundred days that even the gods hid in terror at your sorrow
And the world slept on pretending not to hear or know
Who can face you now that you've survived and seen your tomorrow?

We now sing 'never again' with heads bowed down still
Afraid to look you in the eye and live with what they may reveal
Too scared to face the souls keeping sentinel on top of your every hill

From afar we now stand in hot shame marveling at your rebirth
Wondering how you slew the monster and defied even death
And as we see you rise again, we only watch in awe catching our breath

*Kwibuka is a Rwandan word for "remember"

POEMS FROM THE MALAWIAN WOMEN'S POETRY WORKSHOP

Lost Nation

Agatha Malunda

Rotten meat is been sold in the shops
Who can request for toothpicks these days?
Candy stores are been closed
People are suffering from moral decay
Heaven has lost its eye
Now how will we make hay?
No one wishes to face the blackboard
Teachers are the first to play.

The backbone of our crown is damaged
The king says no to undergo an x-ray.
Our castles' doors are never locked
And I see no guards at the entrance.
Our young birds wish to catch worms
But they never leave their nests early.
Nuns are a ghost in our land
 young women refuse to imitate Mary.

I see old men digging graves
To bury their young bones.
They watered the bush
That kept the eggs of a python.
Now they watch their toddlers
Die of dire venom
our land will come face to face
The fate of Sodom is about.

Silence Kills

Matilda Phiri

I'm too young and beautiful to die
Death is not my near future and not my desire
I'll not remain silent I'll speak out
I can no longer remain victim
Yet I clearly see the light
      Something has to be done
      Something has to change
    Silence destroys, silence kills
I'm for the living and not for the dead
      I'll speak out, I'll speak out

I'm too strong and bold to die
My visions and aspirations await
Why should my future be destroyed?
 I'm I disadvantaged for being a girl?
Is it by choice that I'm an orphan?
Why do you keep abusing me ?
      Today this nonsense must stop
     I'm ever brave,I'm speaking about it
        It's over and over,no more silence

I am too daring and unfit to die
My spear and arrow ready set
 I'll tell the whole world to know
That you want to destroy my future
Soon the court will judge you
You'll leave to regret your evil deeds
The misery of prison awaits your dirty life
I'm so ashamed of your actions.

POEMS FROM THE MALAWIAN WOMEN'S POETRY WORKSHOP

Lady of Letters

Rhoda Zulu

She scribbled what came to mind
As she actively wrote and wrote
Sharp eyed and keen observer
Too strong to be ignored by pen
Drew up curious assorted writings

She was an elected official
Passionately guarded pen and paper
Smelled colonialism, stinking odour
Too vivid to be disregarded by marker
Drew up stories and reported

She loved her native land
But couldn't stand violence
She endured pains and fears
Too strong to be ignored by fountain pen
Contrived for peace and justice

She wasn't conscious of her talent
But she was always in motion
Laid bare hidden cruel evils
Too brutal to be disregarded by ball point
Revealed things as they unfolded

She made life extraordinary
But that she saw with naked eye
Bored with stinky odour, acted
Too obvious to be unnoticed by writers
Brought up by a possessive mother

She loved her home country
But that she hated injustice
That prevailed under selfish rule
Too oppressive to be unscathed by pen
Opened up the world to all

POEMS FROM THE MALAWIAN WOMEN'S POETRY WORKSHOP

Beautiful Little Flower

Luckier Chikopa

I am a beautiful little flower

Everybody wants to have me

I shine at dawn and dusk

But during the day I fill the pain of the sun

When it's sunny nobody is near me

Nobody waters me

Nobody touches me

But this is the time I need people most

I am always thirsty when it's sunny

I always want to shine

My lifespan is too short

I want to see everything

Just like you I have dreams

Please help me to see my dreams

Don't kill me before my time

I am a beautiful little flower

POEMS FROM THE MALAWIAN WOMEN'S POETRY WORKSHOP

Silence

Linly Mayenda

Silence is the communication of the heart
Silence is death
Silence is salvation
Silence

My eyes are filled with sadness
To the world that has covered my heard with disgrace

With your beatings you have silenced me
With your humiliation and embracement
You have mocked me

But will not remain quiet
I will scream even in my whisper

POEMS FROM THE MALAWIAN WOMEN'S POETRY WORKSHOP

The Tools We Carry

Mildred Barya (Instructor)

This happens at Wash Park. Through the sextant's eye, the sun is lime green and sits on top of the lake. Every four seconds it moves. We are still on the bench. Folks come and go. Geese poop, eat, and squirrels pick nuts off the trees. We are here and there, in space and time, measuring distance, speed and altitudes. The man with a red hat next to me tells me it's not the sun that moves but earth rotating. Because the body of earth is huge and we are on it, we don't see it circling the sun but have the image of the sun in motion. This is the magic of science; what is and what appears to be, a source and then the apparent source. I begin to wonder if one could fall asleep and wake up as someone else. A successful simulacrum orbiting without breaking sequence, yet never forgetting what is.

I see the sun and then the sunlight.
Light and the light source all at once.

I'm a friend of fractals keeping in mind the apparent source,
Looking for a man-made refrain that breaks the sequence.

When we say the sun moves from east to west
Where are we (in motion) finding center and decentering?

The Nature of Opposition

Mildred Barya (Instructor)

Jupiter says I'm in the house of endings
The car dies
The man barks
Trees shed their flowerings

I feel like a ghost
To imagine we are all housed in houses
Even when we go into the woods, the seas
Our spirits are still inside some vessel

At some point Jupiter will enter Gemini,
influencing my communication.
Earth will spin between sun and Mars,
but it's my heart's trepidation I will hear.
Mars is very red. Rising at sunset,
it shines brilliantly all night, and could be
mistaken for the sun if night was day.
I wonder if that's how it gets its name—
It impairs the appearance of, the god of war.
What other god mars, spoils, disfigures and
is visible to the naked eye from time to time?

Earth's motion situates Mars opposite the sun
Where astronomers see it clearly and say,
Mars is in opposition to the sun. And us?
Tiny insects in the reel. Yet still,
Imagine our importance in all that.

POEMS FROM THE MALAWIAN WOMEN'S POETRY WORKSHOP

Since You Attended My Funeral, I'll Also Attend Yours

Beverley Nambozo Nsengiyunva (Instructor)

Since you attended my funeral, I'll also attend yours.
I'll arrive just before the coffin
Enters the church
And join the line of weepers.
Weepers, mind you, not mourners.
Weeping is the physical evidence for facebook
That people actually cared about you.

But mourning…
Mourning is the spiritual evidence
That people actually cared about you.

I'll stand with the weepers,
dab my eyelids and sniffle
Make sure I greet the right people.
Your great aunt
The one who hugs me so hard
That she flattens my breasts
I'll hug your grandmother
The one whose weave gets caught in my earrings.
I'll hug your uncle
The one whose hands rest on my bum
Like he's kneading dough.
Since you attended my funeral,
I'll also attend yours.
I'll place a wreath on your coffin
Pluck out the petals and leave the thorns.

I'll deliver a speech
About how close we were as friends
And in the collection box
I'll leave a copy of my HIV results
And a photo of that passionate night.

Published in Expound Magazine, 2016

POEMS FROM THE MALAWIAN WOMEN'S POETRY WORKSHOP

The Other Woman's Tongue

Beverley Nambozo Nsengiyunva (Instructor)

The other woman's tongue
Rolls out like a slide

Her tongue fits in my husband's throat
like a key,
unlocking his little devils.

The little devils
slide down her tongue.

She calls my children to play
But when my children slide down
Her tongue to play,
They hurt themselves and cry.

Marcia Krause Bilyk   DOGWOOD

FICTION

Taking Sides

Jennifer Clements

Hannah knows food. And what was just injected into her sister's feeding tube is nothing of the kind. *Food* is the crunch of a Fuji, the tang of cranberry, the char of BBQ. Hannah wants to shout this at the nurse. She wants to shame the nurse into confessing that the plastic tube cut into her sister's belly for this so-called feeding is an indefensible violation of her remaining hours. Let her feel human. Let her be alive until she isn't. Hannah wants to upset the apple cart, rock the boat, make waves. But Hannah's not like that, so instead of shouting, she watches the nurse tidy up—flushing and capping the feeding tube, stuffing the pop-top can and the bag and the tubing and the syringe and the wipes and the gloves into a bigger bag headed for what must be a stupendous daily accumulation in the bowels of the hospital.

Tubes carrying fluids emerge from under the sheet. As if the room is a small municipality, with conduits for supply and sewerage, power and light, officials who intervene as required. At the center of it, population one, is Annie—the lace straps of her nightgown and her tight black curls, her beatific smile and radiant skin, a madonna.

Hannah touches her sister's arm. "You okay?"

Annie opens her eyes and says, yes, she's okay. She's happy, not in pain. She explains that she's not really in her body.

Where is she if not in her body? Hannah eyes one corner of the ceiling. And what is there to be happy about?

"Everything is different now," says Annie. Her speech is slow and spare, but her eyes are euphoric, like she's just checked the numbers on her lottery ticket three times, and they are still the right ones. "Daddy's here," she says.

But then the door flies open, and it's Jane. She calls across the room to Annie—how is she this beautiful morning? Not waiting for an answer, she says she has really, really good news. She positions herself at the foot of the bed, alert for both her sisters' reactions. She explains that she's gotten Annie accepted for a clinical trial in Boston. She didn't mention it earlier in case it fell through, but as of just a few minutes ago, Annie has the green light. She continues to explain until the words get technical. "You get the picture," she finishes.

Hannah is shocked. Annie leaving here and going to Boston, starting new treatments with new doctors at a new hospital. Are they all going? How soon? Hannah is on break, but classes start again next week. She's teaching Chocolate and Confectionery, and it's a nightmare when somebody else does the first class. She stops herself; how can she be thinking about classes; Annie is what matters. It sounds impossible, getting fragile Annie from here to there. But when Jane has a plan, you don't interfere.

Annie shows neither excitement nor doubt. She's gazing toward a place on the far wall. When Jane stops talking, Annie says, "Anyway. Our father is here. Our father who art in heaven." She laughs. "He's not saying anything. He's just here. Or maybe I'm there. It's kind of both at the same time."

Jane starts to say something, but her phone dings. Shoulder to the wall, she taps the screen.

Hannah says to Annie, "You see Daddy? He's here?"

I know. It's crazy."

Hannah looks to where Annie stares. A picture on the wall of a ship sailing into the wind. Below the picture, an aqua plastic chair piled with clean sheets and a pillow. "It's almost time for the awards ceremony," Annie says.

Jane's phone dings another text.

Annie says that everything is so real where she is. She says it's beyond words. She tries to describe the light, but no, it's more a feeling than a light; it's vivid and joyous and free. She makes a dissatisfied face. "Whatever I say sounds stupid. Do you want me to tell Daddy anything?"

Jane says she has to go. She needs to make arrangements. She steps toward Annie and speaks with a crisp loud voice. "I'm so pleased Boston is happening. You're going to be fine, Annie. We're going to lick this." She pulls the door open and is gone.

Hannah smiles at Annie. The smile says, busy Jane, always a little too serious.

Annie singsongs, "Anna and Hannah split a banana."

Hannah gives the response. "While playing piana for folks in Havana."

"You remember."

"Of course I remember."

They were in the kitchen that Saturday afternoon, Daddy with the two of them, laughing and singing the rhyme they'd just made up. They didn't see Jane until too late. She'd come home early from swim practice and was standing in the doorway, a strand of wet hair wound around two fingers. They stopped singing, and the kitchen went quiet. Their daddy tried to make a rhyme for Jane. Jane on a plane. But Jane ignored him. They listened to her stomping up the two sets of stairs to her attic bedroom. Their father explained that Jane's name didn't rhyme with banana, that her name wasn't silly, and maybe that was just as well since Jane herself wasn't silly. He reminded them that Jane was older and had a serious butterfly collection and read Charlotte Bronte books from the library.

"Just because you're twins doesn't mean you know everything," Jane would scold. But she took care of them. She rescued them from rude boys on the playground; her threats left the boys confounded. When they were accused of stealing in the five and dime, Jane intervened. Then she grew up and became a doctor and was even more formidable.

Annie shifts position in the bed. A streak of pain across her face, as though she's stubbed her toe or hit her funny bone. "I'm going to rest now," she says. She looks for a long time at her sister. "Imagine how it is to be with Daddy." That smile of hers, the freckles, like seeing in a mirror, except her face so much thinner. " Go now," she says. "Find our Jane. Tell her I love her."

Hannah goes down the hall, past elderly ladies in chenille bathrobes and pillow-flattened hair walking laps, pushing IV poles. Empty wheelchairs, carts with dishes covered by napkins. She doesn't want to be here. She doesn't want Annie to be here. She complained all the other times they were here, but those times they got to bring Annie home. She finds Jane by a window that overlooks the freeway. Tiny cars speed people to spa appointments and grocery shopping. Hannah watches until her sister finishes her call.

"That talk about the awards ceremony. And about our father," Jane says. "Annie's hallucinating, of course. I didn't want to say anything in there. She's delusional."

"She doesn't sound delusional."

Jane explains that you can't take what Annie said seriously, that her mind is unreliable. Lack of oxygen, chemical imbalances, medications, lots of reasons. Hannah says she's read that people do sometimes see to the other side when they're dying, and Jane answers that it's wishful thinking, that there's no science behind those claims. Of course it's real, Hannah says, annoyed. There should be double blind studies? With statistical significance? It's like saying love isn't scientific. Of course it isn't. Who cares.

"Hannah." Jane's tone says the conversation is over.

At the elevator, the doors open, and they step in beside a woman and little girl. The girl, who has a bandage over one eye, slips an arm around the woman's leg, and the woman gathers her close. Jane pushes the door-close button and says she's got a date for the arrival in Boston. She only has to set up the transportation.

Hannah smiles at the child. Asks Jane if she's sure going to Boston is the best plan. Jane says what does she mean, and Hannah says that maybe Annie is past the treatment stage. She waves toward Annie's room somewhere above them. After what the doctors said.

The elevator stops, and the woman guides her child out. Jane waits until the doors close and turns to her sister. "It's a choice to live, Hannah. Do you want Annie to die?" She punches at the elevator button. "Can you, for once, accept that I know more than you do about what's wrong with Annie?"

Hannah says nothing. She watches the illuminated numbers of the passing floors. This always happens.

Jane says she will give Hannah a copy of the journal article. A preliminary study shows a fifteen percent occurrence of remission with an admittedly small group in a similar protocol. Impressive, all the same, and definitely worth trying.

Hannah says aren't the treatments dangerous, and Jane says that Annie is dying and they probably don't need to worry about killing her. They can still win this war. No, no, says Hannah; that's not at all what she meant. Moving Annie out of her bed is what seems dangerous. Making her suffer. Causing her pain. And Annie said nothing about wanting this. Doesn't she get to have an opinion?

They get to the main floor. A man with crutches is waiting, and they hold the doors for him. Walking down the hall, Jane speaks more confidentially, saying that Annie made it clear just now that she's no longer able to make decisions. It's up to them, what happens next. And Hannah doesn't understand how lucky they are that Jane got Annie into this study. There's a long list of people who want in.

Going through the cafeteria line, a woman with a hair net puts the enchilada plate on Hannah's tray. It looks better than mac & cheese or pasta salad—everything is carbs, and that's probably what people here crave. Hannah takes a bundle of silverware. Her sister is dying. At the register, Jane insists on paying, then leads the way to a table by the window. Following, Hannah thinks how wrong it is to put Annie through more treatment. But it's Hannah against Jane. And Jane is always right; Hannah has had zero success disagreeing with Jane about anything. Besides, she knows how it is when Jane gets angry. The time Annie shamed Jane into sharing her magic set when the cousins came to visit, and they broke the top hat. Jane was mad for months; she may still be mad. Hannah's not sure she can take that. She's losing Annie; she needs to keep Jane.

But she can't ignore what she knows. She unrolls the bundle, and with the fork and the knife she nudges the two enchiladas apart. She makes a division; she draws a line.

Tiferet

"I was thinking," she says to Jane. "I was thinking that actually this might be the time for Hospice."

"Are you kidding? Giving up? Now that she's accepted for the trial? That's insane."

"No more tests. No more chemo. I watched the feeding tube thing this morning. It's stupid, doing that."

"I totally disagree with you."

Hannah wants to stop right there, to run away, but instead she gets a brochure from her bag. "'Hospice affirms life,'" she reads. "'Hospice does not hasten death; it provides a painless, fear-free way to die.'" To Jane she says, "It's not a war. Who wants to die in battle?" She holds out the brochure. Then she sets it on the table by Jane's tray. She watches her hands cutting the enchiladas into pieces that look like body parts.

"Hannah," her sister finally says. "I've arranged for the most advanced, the very latest and best treatment for our dying sister. It's the only chance she's got. It could be a cure. How would you live with yourself if down the line, they decide it's the cure they've been searching for? This decision is more complicated than you know."

"What I know is Annie. And I know you're wrong."

"I'm trying to save Annie's life."

"You're trying to do things your own way like you always have. You're doing this for you, not for her." Hannah flutters her hands toward the ceiling. "Being the savior."

Hannah feels a rush of hatred toward her sister. People who hate do unconscionable things. She knows she's trying to do things her own way just as much as her sister is. But right beside the hatred, sharing breath with it, there's a feeling that no matter what happens, for once she's done and said what she needed to. That counts for something. She stands. Picks up her tray with the dissected enchiladas. "I have to get back upstairs."

* * *

It's not hard to tell. She's dead.

The body on the bed with its tubes and attachments is empty. The occupant has packed her bags and left. Hannah isn't ready for this; they only went for lunch; there's more she meant to say. Did Annie do this on purpose? Is it because of Jane's plan? Or did she just want to do it when she was alone; you read about that. Annie is dead. Just say it, no euphemisms. She didn't *go* or pass away or give up the ghost. This can't be happening. Annie, come back! Hannah stands by the bed, waiting for the wave of grief that will drag her under. But instead there's an unexpected still moment when she has a choice about how she will react.

Surprised, almost guilty, Hannah watches bereft make way for curious.

Something has been left behind. Evidence of the departure. Annie has slipped through a portal, and the hatch is still propped open. There's a sweet smell, and it's as if the sun is shining, flooding the room, but not from outside the window, and you can't really see it, but even so it's incredibly bright. Hannah knows this makes no sense and that maybe it's some wrinkle in her sanity, but it's very real. Best of all, Annie is not gone; Hannah is certain that she still exists somewhere, and she's in touch, and everything's okay, more than okay. Annie's being in that state takes Hannah there too. The curiosity and the surprise and the joy make her laugh.

Jane looks at her as if she's lost it. "What?"

"Annie's happy."

"Annie's dead."

Hannah will not argue. And she's thought of something else. She asks if Jane remembers the awards ceremony, the years-ago one. Jane does not until Hannah reminds her it was at the science fair Jane won in ninth grade, something with fruit flies, and then Jane smiles and says she was so proud of winning, and wonders why Annie's wandering brain chose now to pull that up.

When Hannah says she thinks it was Annie's way of explaining where she was going, Jane's smile turns skeptical and she asks why they are talking about science fairs when their sister has just died. Hannah asks if that's what Jane wants, that they stop talking? Jane shrugs and says it's okay, just not to tell her about how Annie has been borne aloft on angels' wings.

Hannah says that the awards ceremony night was their birthday, hers and Annie's. She was making dinner from their mother's Julia Child cookbook. Artichokes with hollandaise, boeuf Bourguignon. Those old recipes. Whisks and double-boilers and eggshells all over the kitchen counter. She'd made a bittersweet chocolate cake. Then Jane had announced their daddy was going to her awards ceremony. No, they had said, it was their birthday; there was the dinner. Jane and Annie got into a big fight about it.

Hannah realizes where this is headed, but she can't stop now. She says their daddy gave the twins a lecture before they got in the car. Saying he hadn't known about the ceremony either, but they all needed to be generous. Explaining endlessly how important this was to Jane. "The message was that you mattered more."

Jane shakes her head. "The message was that he loved you more, and he had to make up for it."

Hannah focuses on straightening the twisted strap of Annie's nightgown. Flattens it against her sister's bony shoulder.

Jane says she was only going to win the award that one night, and Annie and Hannah could do their fancy dinner another time. It was just for the family.

Hannah says it was a big deal to her, it mattered, and Jane delivers a chilly apology; she's sorry she wrecked their birthday party. Hannah says it wasn't just that night; Jane was the leader, and the twins were to follow. "You know what Annie's last words were? That she loved you."

"Fantastic. She's gone straight to heaven. I'm still the monster." Jane's eyes fill. "I was so jealous of you two. Everybody loved you. You loved everybody. The adorable twins."

Hannah remembers the sound of Jane's feet going up the stairs the night of the rhyme. She says it never looked that way. It looked like Jane was always the winner and always knew the answers, and Hannah was afraid to disagree with her. "I'm still afraid." Hannah smooths wrinkles out of the sheet over Annie's chest.

"Afraid of me? That's a little hard to believe."

Hannah says she was supposed to agree to whatever Jane came up with. That was her job. It feels like because she's telling Jane now, that she'll hate her, and she doesn't want Jane to hate her. Hannah works her hand in under Annie's fingers.

"What am I supposed to say to you, Hannah? Am I supposed to apologize for who I am?"

"I'm not sure. Am I?"

Jane puts one hand on her pocket with the phone. "We need to call the funeral home."

"No. It's too soon, and I'm not ready. Annie's not ready. Look at her face."

"That's nonsense, Hannah. She's dead. I'm calling the funeral home."

"See. This is what you do. You bully me."

Looking down at Annie, Hannah is again drawn into the impossible to explain the feeling that for right now, everything is profoundly okay. The thing with Jane. Even losing her twin. She closes Annie's fingers around her own.

Standing on the opposite side of the bed, arms on the rail, Jane watches. She reaches to stroke Annie's forehead, her fingers disappearing into Annie's curls. Then takes her sisters' hands in her own. She says, "Annie's dead. And I was too busy to say goodbye."

The tubes entering and exiting from under the sheet, the glass of water with the bent straw, the plant from the shop downstairs and the picture of a sailing ship, the wipes, swabs, tissues, lotion—none of it serves a purpose any longer. It's like they've already gone decades forward, and this room is an old paper photo in their family album. But standing across from each other, hands clasped, with their sister between, one of them smiles, and the other weeps; it's not a bad way to begin.

NONFICTION

Why Poetry for Difficult Times?

Roger Housden

An Excerpt from *Ten Poems for Difficult Times* by Roger Housden

In his bestselling *Ten Poems* series, author Roger Housden has shown an uncanny ability to choose and discuss poems that strike at the core of readers' concerns and needs. In his latest volume entitled *Ten Poems for Difficult Times*, ten extraordinary poems, along with Housden's incisive essays, bring heartfelt insight and broad perspective both to our personal challenges and to our cultural and collective malaise. We hope you'll enjoy this excerpt from the book.

###

Poetry is a concise and elemental means of expressing the deepest of human emotions: joy, sorrow, grief, hope, love, and longing. It connects us as a people and a community; it speaks for us in a way few other forms of writing can do. When I was in the process of moving to Manhattan in 2001, in the weeks after 9/11, poems appeared on every available wall in the city. Yet even though I was so aware of poetry's power, over the next ten years, while sitting alone in front of my computer, finishing up another volume in my Ten Poems series, I would wonder at times whether I was wasting my time.

After all, the world is in trouble. It has always been in trouble. Not only that, but we are often in trouble personally, too. Surely there must be something more useful, more pressing, to give my time to than reflecting on poetry? Couldn't I go start a project in Africa, or at least do some small thing to prevent climate catastrophe, start reducing my own carbon footprint, for example, and begin a movement to encourage others to do the same? But no; I wrote more poetry books, wondering all the while whether they and I were doing little more than making ourselves progressively irrelevant.

I knew better, which is why I kept writing. I knew that great poetry has the power to start a fire in a person's life. It can alter the way we see ourselves. It can change the way we see the world. You may never have read a poem in your life, and yet you can pick up a volume, open it to any page, and suddenly find yourself blown into a world full of awe, dread, wonder, marvel, deep sorrow, and joy. Poetry not only matters; it is profoundly necessary. *Especially* in times of darkness and difficulty, both personal and collective. To read or write poetry is a powerful, even subversive, act, and it is one small thing we can do that can make a very big difference.

It can make a difference because at its best poetry calls forth our deep Being, bids us to live by its promptings. It dares us to break free from the safe strategies of the cautious mind, from our default attitudes and beliefs. It calls to us, like the wild geese, as Mary Oliver would say, from an open sky. It is a magical art, and always has been — a making of language spells designed to open our eyes, open our doors, and welcome us into a bigger world, one of possibilities we may never have dreamed of. This is also why poetry can be dangerous: we may never be the same again after reading a poem that speaks to our own life directly. I know that when I meet my own life in a great poem, I feel opened, clarified, confirmed, somehow, in what I always sensed was true but had no words for. Anything that can do this is surely necessary for the fullness of a human life.

The word *poet* means a "maker" — someone who crafts language into a shape. The word *maker* has the same etymological root as the words *matrix*, and *magic*, and it's true that the sound, the rhythm, of good poetry is literally spellbinding. It lulls, it sways, it rises and falls, and our hearts and minds rise and fall along with it. Poetry literally entrains us into the energy, the mood, the vibration, even, that the poet conjures with her words and images. The subtler and more refined that energy is, the more it can raise us to the best that we are. That it does so is another reason poetry is so necessary today, when we need our best selves more than ever.

Poetry revitalizes our imagination. A hundred years ago, when Yeats was alive, the imagination was far more of a common currency than it is today. The imagination today is under siege. Our political leaders, steeped in doublespeak and alternative facts, have brought George Orwell's *1984* closer than ever. We are saturated with both false and genuine information and find it a challenge to tell the difference. We are saturated with concepts and opinions that stream ready-formed from Facebook or Twitter, which siphon our attention into an abstract metaworld divorced from concrete reality. People engage less and less with the natural environment, less and less with each other in community, relying more and more for their experience on the received knowledge that comes on a screen or down a wire.

Tiferet

No wonder the imagination is in danger of shriveling to the size of a pea. Imagination feeds on the smell of old tree roots, on conversation, on barking dogs, on the cries of children. Poetry's fuel is the imagination; it uses the things of this concrete world for its material and then reaches down into the layers of meaning that any object or person contains. Pablo Neruda wrote an ode to a lemon, to his socks, to laziness, to a tomato, to salt, and more. Poetry shows us that not just the gods but the humblest forms in the world can reveal enough truth and beauty to fill us with praise and awe.

Poetry rescues the world from oblivion by the practice of attention. Our attention honors and gives value to living things, gives them their proper name and particularity, retrieves them from the obscurity of the general. When I pay attention, something in me awakens, and that something is much closer to who I am than the driven or drifting self I usually take myself to be. When I pay attention, I am straightened, somehow, brought into a deeper life.

Poetry takes a stand against the increasing homogenization of world cultures because it is the speech of one specific individual in his unique voice. The sweeping homogenization and commodification of everything may be one reason that there are more poetry festivals, slams, groups, readings, and creative writing courses than ever before. Poetry is the expression of one person's irreplaceable subjective sensibility, another name for which is *soul*. It is the creation of one sensibility, giving form to how it feels to be oneself and to see the world through one's own eyes in the most precise language one can summon.

Everyday language usually fails to do this well. But poetry reaches with its sounds and rhythms down below the realm of the conscious mind to awaken and nourish the imagination. Poetry is imagination's language, and as such, it is prophetic speech. In essence, what is found there is our deep humanity, which binds us in empathy for others, however different they may appear to be from us. In everyday language, we might say to someone, for example, "I feel sick," which doesn't tell the listener very much and doesn't allow her to feel very much. But the poet Robert Lowell says it this way:

I hear my ill spirit sob in each blood cell

Poetry says the unsayable. Lowell makes clear the nature of his sickness; it is a sickness of soul, one that pervades the body. And as the poet Mark Doty observes in the essay "Why Poetry Matters Now," Lowell's sickness sobs, and the sobbing is accentuated by the twelve vowels in that sentence, the alliteration of the *b*s and the *l*s. All this makes the line thick and heavy in the mouth, Doty says, which is what sobbing does. Try saying it, and see what a mouthful it is. Lowell gives us the visceral experience, not just the information that he is sick.

Lowell's line comes from the idiosyncratic stuff of his selfhood — from the unique soul of Lowell. Someone else would speak to sickness in a different way. Here is Sylvia Plath on having a fever:

I am a lantern —
My head a moon
Of Japanese paper. My gold beaten skin
Infinitely delicate and infinitely expensive.

The metaphors come tumbling over one other. She steps out of her body, it seems, and makes of it something other — a lantern, which then becomes something other — a moon.

This is a long way from Lowell, but it's another world altogether from the blunt vagueness of "I feel sick." The difference between the two poets is one of voice. And by the writer's voice we mean the way the particular texture of subjective perception finds its way into speech.

Who knows how the image of a lantern came to Plath. She likely didn't know. Poems are a window into the soul because they honor the unknown, both in us and in the world. They come from the deep waters below the surface; they are shaped into form by the power of language and set free to fly with wings of images and metaphor. Imagine a world in which everything was already known. It would be a dead world, no questions, no wonder, no other possibilities. That's what my own world can feel like sometimes when my imagination has gone into retreat. I, like you, no doubt, have discovered that poetry is a phoenix I can fly on to return to that forgotten land.

Poetry uses words that are known to all of us but in a sequence and order that surprises us out of our normal speech rhythms and linear thought processes. Poetry uniquely combines imaginative power and conscious intelligence, inspiration and hard work, and its effect is to illuminate our lives and breathe new life, new seeing, new tasting into the world we thought we knew. Poetry bids us to eat the apple whole.

Poems like the ones in this book shake me awake. They pass on their attentiveness, their insight, their love of this broken world to me, the reader. We can wake up to the world and to ourselves in a new way by reading poems such as these — especially when we read them aloud, and shape the sounds on our lips and the rhythms on our breath — making us more fully human. The poet Jane Hirshfield says, "Whether from reading the New England Transcendentalists or Eskimo poetry, I feel that everything I know about being human has been deepened by the poems I've read."

John Keats speaks of this humanizing power, too, when he says, "Poetry should strike the reader as a wording of his own highest thoughts, and appear almost as a Remembrance."

That's all very well, you might say. Poems may be a humanizing influence, they may even carry us to the heights of spiritual insight and realization, but what have they done to shift the world's obsession with power, greed, and violence? What has a poem done to dissolve injustice? This argument has been rising and falling for centuries, but it is worth our notice that poetry and literature in general have been routinely banned around the world at various times because of their subversive influence. If poetry and literature are humanizing influences, they work directly against those regimes and ideologies that restrict rather than encourage liberty and justice. Nazim Hikmet, whose poem "It's This Way" is in this book, spent eighteen years in a Turkish prison for his beliefs. Because poetry connects different worlds, different ideas, and different people and things, it generates empathy — empathy with others and with all living things. When, through a poetic act of imagination, one feels kinship with others and with all life, it is that much more difficult to oppress others; and that, in a tyrannical regime, is subversion.

Stalin tried to strip Russia of its soul with his death camps. Poet Osip Mandelstam restored that soul by reciting poetry to his fellow convicts and by writing about it in his journal. "Perhaps to remain a poet in such circumstances," Saul Bellow writes, "is also to reach the heart of politics. The human feelings, human experiences, the human form and face, recover their proper place — the foreground."

That, after all, is what politics is ultimately about — human feelings and the human form. Poetry can give a human face to our collective struggles and remind us that this human world is not only broken, it is beautiful. That is what the poems in this volume do. There's a headstone in a Long Island graveyard — the one where Jackson Pollock is buried — that I think encapsulates the value and necessity of poetry in a world of sorrows: "Artists and poets are the raw nerve ends of humanity. By themselves they can do little to save humanity. Without them there would be little worth saving."

# # #

Excerpted from the book *Ten Poems for Difficult Times*. Copyright ©2018 by Roger Housden. Printed with permission from New World Library — www. newworldlibrary.com.

NONFICTION

The Scholarship Ceremony

Emma Margraf

It was the fourth scholarship ceremony in a week. You'd taken off work, smiled, and shaken everyone's hand. You'd repeated the same things about how great it was that Jez was going to college and answered the same damn questions about what a difference the $500, $750, $1000 and $4000 checks were going to make in Jez's life more times than you could count. There were catered meals with plastic pitchers of water and silver baskets of rolls in crisp white napkins. The meals were always chicken.

You never spent much time eating. You answered questions. Your job was to assure people they'd made a solid investment. You made them feel good about their generosity. It was a job you did well. It was a job you were almost done with. The end felt so tantalizingly close.

Each conversation was the same. You said that everything counted so much for her. You explained that the money was going towards things like books and supplies and housing costs, which she wouldn't be able to afford otherwise. It was incredibly generous of the foundation/the donors/the state to support her. Yes, she plans to live in the dorms and study psychology, yes, she would like to mentor at-risk youth. Yes, it is so great that she wants to give back. No, you've never seen the Sandra Bullock movie. You nodded your head a lot just like the social workers did.

This event was the big one. They were in a beautiful theater on an expensive private school college campus. There were large oak trees and manicured walkways with donor labeled benches. Neither of them had been there before. The buildings were stone, and cold. There were elected officials, news reporters, and cameras hired to capture the special moment when this year's group of wards of the state received the governor's scholarship for foster youth.

Jez was on the stage with a former governor, who said to her, "well, you must have had a whole lot of people who helped you get to this place of success! Tell us about those people."

Jez responded by pointing at you and saying, "no it was pretty much just her," and then stayed uncharacteristically quiet. You knew that wasn't what the former governor wanted to hear, so you jumped in and nervously added, "Oh, don't be silly, there were lots of great teachers, like Mr. Mo at Montessori?"

The former governor looked quizzically at you.

You were supposed to say that these kids flourish in public school. You were supposed to say that public school teachers are heroes. You were supposed to have a story about a math teacher who went the extra mile to make sure this one kid would not fall through the cracks. You were not supposed to say that public school let her down, that the teachers there did her damage, and that she'd run from it desperate for an alternative. You were supposed to be grateful.

Better not to stick around for any more questions. No questions about why public school was the worst, how they got funding for private school, no questions. You pulled Jez by the arm off the stage with a flurry of thank yous and big smiles, only to be greeted by a gaggle off stage left that you weren't prepared for. An officer from a philanthropic foundation looked at you and asked, "What's it like to be a foster parent?"

"What's it like? Well it's certainly a challenge, but with the help of a solid community —"

"No what's it *really* like?" she asked with a laughably serious look on her face. "You've performed miracles with these children, and people would love to know what you really go through." The words felt like slow motion punches. Everyone always wanted to talk about miracles. There were no miracles. It was hard, sad, alienating work that made these people feel like strangers to you.

You shifted your weight back and forth from one foot to another. You couldn't tell her the truth, and making a joke like that your favorite parenting moment was teaching Jez to hang a spoon on her nose probably wouldn't go over with this crowd. You and Jez lived in a small town. The impact of truth or bad jokes would be felt in whispers that would result in unpredictable consequences.

It had been a long day already. You and Jez had been late to get there, gotten lost on the way, and not known where to park. The gaslight was on in the car. You'd been given the wrong name for the building you were supposed to go to, and you had only been able to figure it out when you saw the caterers setting up the food for after the ceremony. You'd run in hurriedly, looking behind you to be sure Jez was following along, you'd put your hand on your chest to make sure your phone was in your bra where you usually stuck it, your other hand sticking your keys in the outside pocket of your purse. You dodged catering trays to the left and to right of the door to the ceremony. Jez had never seen caterers in white before.

"What's it really like?"

Tiferet

Your eyes started to lose focus.

What it's really like.

Well, you have a child, in your living room. You don't know anything about them, from what gender they identify with to what their educational skills are to what happened to their parents. What you do know is that you have a plastic bag full of medicines in your hand with a list of instructions for this child, who you don't really know at all but are suddenly totally in charge of. What's most pressing is that it's 9pm on a Sunday night and this child is here with their possessions in large garbage bags and you, you have no idea what they even like to eat for breakfast.

You think you can run to the store, but you aren't allowed to leave this child alone for any amount of time per court order, so your neighbor comes to the rescue with a box of Cinnamon Toast Crunch and some milk that the child seems to be happy about. You do your best to get organized, make a plan, get a schedule together.

Your days are filled with bullshit. You take this child to school every day and pick them up, you sign school forms that you don't know for sure you have permission to sign, you break rules that you didn't even know were rules that existed to break. You go to parent-teacher conferences and get stared at by teachers and counselors who automatically expect you to take every damn word they say as the absolute truth even though you don't know what the truth is, and maybe you will never know.

You ask yourself how these teachers could be so sure that this child can't go to college. You never thought you'd find yourself hating teachers. You ask yourself how they know it was this child who threatened other kids in the hallway and *why* this child would have done that. You know that no adult witnessed this crime, and that the school had already decided what happened.

You argue with people. You cajole. You negotiate to get this child into summer camps, tutoring programs, therapy with a specialist, music programs, theater programs, whatever. You argue with school counselors who tell you that college prep classes are a waste for these kinds of kids. You take yes for an answer. People keep things from you because they don't want to hear it anymore. You've become that person. You are bossy.

You find yourself looking at all of the kids on the street and wondering what you don't know. Who knows their real story? Who knows anyone's? You have this one kid who is going to college and that's supposed to mean what? Has all of the work you've done been worth it?

You hate the word miracle. You worked at a plan for seven years to get this child into college, and the child worked hard, too. You both encountered people at every turn that said, 'these kids don't graduate from high school,' or 'these kids aren't cut out for an education,' and sometimes those are words you hear from powerful people and you wonder, do they know something you don't?

There was silence in the room that you suddenly heard.

Jez was fidgeting in her dress and elbowing you in the stomach at the same time.

"Mama, are you going to answer her?" Jez was being sweeter than she'd been in the car, when you'd had a fight and Jez told you to shut up.

"Yes. What was the question?" You smiled. But the foundation officer had wandered away and so did Jez, heading for the food and the other kids.

You stood by yourself, scanning the landscape, and got your phone out of your bra to check the time. A man in a suit passed you by and gave you a look as your hand went under your shirt. Right. That's what you notice.

This isn't how this was supposed to be. You imagined, you had dreams, you had visions of what was going to happen when you took in or were an advocate for kids who you knew you could help. Some of it turns out the way you thought it would. Some of it doesn't. When you first started, you had dreams of appearing at fundraisers with kids who'd turned into success stories, whose growth was impossible to miss and who endeared themselves to masses of people. Their appearances would turn people onto the idea that everyone was worth paying attention to. But you seemed to always be advocating for kids whom no one was interested in hearing about.

Jez was the closest exception. Everyone wanted to hear just a little bit from her. They were so surprised that this child who was awkward, always said the wrong thing, and spoke too loudly graduated from high school and got into college. It was the opposite of what they expected from the world. Excitement with thinly veiled anxiety.

"Wow, did you ever expect this could happen?"

"Was everyone surprised?"

"How did you pull this off?"

"Do you think it's a lot of money to spend — going to college?"

And your favorite: "Does she know how lucky she is?"

The truth was that Jez wasn't, and would likely never, be fucking lucky. And the idea that after all she been through and worked for, acceptance to a state school with a moderate scholarship qualified as luck was laughable. Some days and some conversations were so preposterous that you imagined squirting the person in the face with squirt guns or hitting them with a whipped cream pie.

Tiferet

The moment Jez got into college was a sweet one. She couldn't bring herself to read the letter, so she handed it to you, and you read it out loud. When she got her driver's license, she could hardly wait to tell you. She'd memorized sixty-eight lines of Shakespeare for the eighth grade play. She'd learned to swim and to navigate all over town. She'd passed physics and learned to jump rope. She was really good at the spoon thing, and had made you a card for Mother's Day that was an ode to your love of mushrooms. You thought it was hilarious. It read, "Happy Mother's Day! Let's mushroom it up!"

You'd spent most of the last eight years listening to people lie to you. Kids lied to you. Social workers lied to you. Lawyers, police officers, foundation officers, teachers, principals, and administrators lied to you about what was legal, what was possible, what kids had done and what they hadn't, what you were allowed to do and what you weren't. They spent years telling you what was accepted as true but actually wasn't so often that you had a hard time believing anyone at all.

The car ride home was quiet but for the radio. You wait in traffic most of the way, turning a forty-five minute drive into a ninety-minute one. When you pulled up, Jez's seat belt was off before you had a chance to take the keys out of the ignition. She ran into the house ahead of you. You walked slowly up the stairs and kicked off your shoes when you walked in the door. You turned to the cabinet and picked up a rocks glass, walked back to your room, pulled a bottle of whiskey out of the closet, poured yourself an inch of it, and lay down on your bed. Your phone was ringing, but you didn't look at it. Jez called saying that she'd locked the front door and turned out the lights, and you said fine. The sky got darker.

You had wondered what the edge looked like. You broke many rules. You made a lot of enemies. You knew a lot of kids. You never thought about whether you would do this forever or for just a few more years. Now seemed like a perfectly good time to leave. No more paperwork. No more rules. You'd start looking for a new life. You might get a dog. You might go to grad school. You might.

You would never take another kid. But the story doesn't end there.

Nature, Nukes and the Search for Inner (and Outer) Peace: An Interview with John Brantingham

Stephanie Barbé Hammer

1. Mazel Tov on your being named the first ever Sequoia and Kings Canyon National Parks Poet Laureate for 2018-19 (is that right or is it a 2 year tenure?) Please tell us a little about how that nomination happened and what you hope to do during your tenure.

No one has really defined the length of it [yet!] I'd be happy living in this position for the rest of my life because it really represents one of my greatest dreams. I love Sequoia and Kings Canyon. I've spent most summers and many winters there since 1976 – which means probably that I've been out there as much or more than anyone except for some of the long-time rangers.

The nomination came after I had volunteered there for 4 1/2 years. As we enter our 5th year of volunteer-work my wife Ann and I plan to continue teaching week-long poetry and art classes outside in the parks. These classes are free, as is the camping. It's a fantastic experience, and I've loved seeing so many people grow through this program. I've grown too. There's something about being off grid and seriously talking about art with artists in this beautiful place that cannot be replicated.

During the coming year I want to keep teaching of course and I want to start teaching in new ways. If I can work out a way to teach online, I will. That might be through Inlandia Institute out in Riverside California. I love what they do. Additionally, I hope to develop an anthology for people who have written about the park and continue to do so. And of course, I will continue to write about the parks. Finally, I want time just to wander and write about what it means to be a part of nature.

Tiferet

On our first day in the mountains I always tell students the following: the forest is not the trees or the animals or any individual thing. It is a context and once you enter the forest, you become a part of that context; once you enter the forest, you are the forest, and that it takes a while to become aware of that, but that awareness is a profound epiphany that cannot be fully described. We try to approximate and share it though in our poetry. That is the joy of the place: that moment of spiritual growth when you find the deep interconnection between yourself and the world.

2. You and I and interfaith blogger/author Larry Behrendt have talked a lot about our religious backgrounds and journeys. I know that you were raised a Catholic. Would you tell us a bit about how you came to associate with the Friends, and how your view of yourself as an artist and as a human being has changed/evolved through that process?

Yes, I was actually raised between those worlds. I was a Catholic, but my father was a Friend, and I was always fascinated by it. I agreed with the passion and the ideas of the Friends. I never really attended meetings until I was in my forties, but I was drawn in by their ideas of nonviolence, and the idea that God lives in all of us.

That's the truth I find in the forest every time. God is not some abstraction. God is the interconnectedness that makes every moment sacred if you can see it. It's there and easy to find in the forest, but it is just as present in my classroom and even at the DMV. It takes some restructuring to see, but it's there.

3. I'm very curious about your just published book about nuclear dread, *A Sublime and Tragic Dance* with images by Kendall Johnson. How did this work come to be? You mention in your intro that you and Ken were both fascinated by Oppenheimer? My question for you there is why? What was so interesting about him to you?

What drew me in was that Oppenheimer took a scientific and philosophical approach to the study of nature. He became a kind of sorcerer in the end because he understood something fundamental about the way the universe was put together. He represents a kind of shadow side of what I hope to do, but he approached the natural world in a lot of ways in the same way that I do. He would take off into the deserts of New Mexico on a horse by himself seeking wildness and thunderstorms. I do that too; I love being in those High Sierra thunderstorms. It's a potentially dangerous pastime maybe, but there is so much energy there that it's addictive.

Oppenheimer was a monster and a genius --someone who strove to both be a saint and deeply human, and I think to understand him is to understand something fundamental about what it means to be us. His work killed so many people and yet he also fought to eliminate nuclear weapons. He committed two attempted murders and at the same time he tried to help people understand physics and the beauty of the natural world. His energy must have been enormous. I am disgusted by him and fascinated at the same time.

4. What are you hoping to get readers to think about with this difficult and terrifying subject?

I am always bothered by the "greater good" kinds of arguments that come with a discussion of Oppenheimer. People often say that the other bombings caused more destruction than the nuclear bombs we dropped on Hiroshima and Nagasaki. That's factually correct, but so what? I don't think those other moments of human destruction were necessary either. Other people argue that it ended the war more quickly. So would have diplomacy. Others say that the Japanese deserved it and acted monstrously. I think that's true too. We were all complicit in the pointless horror and devastation of that time. Nothing justifies holocaust, and I would like to move to a world where people stop making arguments that one nightmare is all right because worse nightmares exist.

5. My favorite poem in the new collection is "The Dripping Season," because it epitomizes what I think are your passions as a poet. Thinking simultaneously big and small, universally and very personally, you elegize the mysteriousness of nature in a very specific way. What's your favorite poem in the collection?

Thank you. I think "The Dripping Season" is my favorite too. It's the one I find myself thinking about the most. I love the feeling I had while writing that this is not the end. Even if I am wiped away, even if the apocalypse comes, there will be something that happens the moment after the apocalypse. I was thinking about Elizabeth Bishop's poem "One Art" as I wrote this. I have lost so much in my life. No more than anyone else, but I am going to lose this world as well, and that's all right. The end of something, even me, is implied by its beginning and that ending can be beautiful if you understand it not least because it leads to something new.

I love nurse trees -- trees that have fallen over and provide the nutrients necessary for new saplings -- so new growth springs out of them. In Sequoia, you can see long rows of giant sequoias that sprang out of nurse trees that decomposed thousands of years ago. The end of one tree implied the beginnings of new trees, and their ends are implied now along with generations of trees that will spiderweb from the first mothers.

That feeling is what I love about that poem.

6.   You are a devoted and passionate teacher. Is teaching as important to you as writing? Or is it important in a different way? How are your laureate-ship, your new book project and your walking project connected to teaching? In what way(s) are these connected to your practice of pacifism? What are you hoping to share, both as a living breathing poet, and as a legacy?

I see all of it as being interconnected. My passion is being able to go more deeply into the self to find what is sacred there and to help others to do the same. If I have a legacy, it is to help people wipe away the ego, which makes us hate each other and ourselves. It would be to be able and to enable others to see the childishness of cynicism and to stop making excuses for our monstrousness. If I had a legacy it would be to help people see that once we enter the forest, we are the forest, and in fact the forest is with us everywhere we go and that every moment can be sacred. We just need to see it.

POETRY

This House . . . Sans Her Spirit

Adrian Ernesto Cepeda

"I knew nothing but shadows and I thought them to be real."
- Oscar Wilde

All the glasses you displayed
now glow half empty thirsting
for you like the walls hearing
the tiles are now much to quiet
so used to hear your midnight
shuffling with chanclas, socks
in slippers, opening cupboards
that miss your touch, even
the couches long for your light
weight, still waiting to save
you a seat. The carpet misses
your footprints, the doors never
want to reopen again, staying
locked inside with all the memories
and you hold the keys, this casa
is the essence of you, your house
is missing your presencia. When
I listen to the painting you picked
Out for the la pared, they whisper
exhibiting so little color in voices
telling me we can hear the sink drips
most nights, showers this palace
with sadness, Mami we keep waiting
for your reawakening, the plants
miss the way you spoke life to root
now wilting, do you miss your leaves?
This stillness much tooa quiet

Tiferet

without your spirit, even the foundation
grass is drying tears, cactus cries
longing for your quintessence
this valiant estate actually perceives—
su casa once glowed silently
can you feel behind these gates
your palacio privately grieve?

Stuart Schaefer   LONGSHADOW

POETRY

Backyard Divination

Tom Plante

Oak saplings cut last fall
when I trimmed the hedges
lay scattered where I left them.
Stripped of leaves, the sticks

are good for kindling and useful
as tomato plant stakes
in this summer's garden.
Their random pattern recalls

the yarrow stalks of the *I Ching*,
a practice I tried to understand
but abandoned when I was young.
These dry sticks are rearranged

by squirrels and sparrows that
come to feed. The north wind
bites the saplings' bark
and scatters ancient clues.

POETRY

From Here to Wherever

Emily Vogel

Shift. Identity or dishes
to the dishes rack.
This late swarming of June light
is going to murder me.
Shift. The children's clothes
from the dryer to their drawers
or the entire entity of myself
from room to room
gathering debris or Holy stones.
What cornerstone might have the builder
attributed to me?
The Lord said, original sin
means you must crawl on your belly
and eat dirt. My daughter
was drinking a juice box beside me
when this was mentioned in church today.
I can't be certain that I am good.
But I washed the upholstery today
with soap and water. Shift.
Once I was a paper-doll
with a throbbing heart
and a dangerous car. The desk
which upheld my language
was left in my spinster's apartment
so long ago
that I cannot recall my life
prior to the shift. I have shifted
the weekly trash into an ordering.
I have shifted my soul
into something ambitiously sane.
But there is yet the felling of trees
in windstorms, and the insane
cacophony of birds. I shift
like an eternal awakening
and the world insists
that I never cease to awaken.
But this is love. I awaken

Tiferet

and get down to business.
A drifting in and out of sleep though,
the baseball fans cheering
and the snap of the bat
always makes me want more,
no matter how wrong, no matter how
out of the element
to which I must submit. And at night,
my children are the wild stars
that shift, as if the light of silent tears,
soft ribboning of light in the sky.
Something for the oblivious
not to notice, when compared
to the perfect BOOK
of another starry language,
the typeset like squid-ink,
set permanent and radiant.
My children on the periphery
of the playground, singing
to the trees.

A Review of

James Wright: A Life in Poetry by Jonathan Blunk

BY ANDREW KAUFMAN

JAMES WRIGHT: A LIFE IN POETRY
By Jonathan Blunk
Farrar, Straus and Giroux
512 Pages
$18.00 Paperback

ISBN: 978-1-947896-01-7
To order: https://www.amazon.com/James-Wright-Poetry-Jonathan-Blunk/dp/0374178593/ref=sr_1_1?ie=UTF8&qid=1534714319&sr=8-1&keywords=james+wright+a+life+in+poetry

This book should be celebrated long into the future as one of the great literary biographies ever produced by our or any other generation. In the interest of clarity, it's reductive even to call this a "biography," as it would be to call Hamlet a murder story. Blunk reveals not only the circumstances of James Wright's day-to-day life, but often his hour-to-hour consciousness, with almost implausible clarity. He shows how Wright's unshakable, at times literally life-and-death obsession with writing led him to produce some of the best American poetry of the past half-century, at least. Blunk portrays this obsession as it takes the form of endless writing, drafting, and re-writing; ceaseless devotion to studying, broadening, and deepening his command of craft; and the seemingly limitless reading of poetry from every conceivable epoch and tradition. Another measure of Wright's compulsion turns out to be his prodigious memory for much or most of what he read, which enabled him to select and recite endless pages of poetry and fiction at will. But as Blunk likewise shows, Wright also struggled throughout with severe depression that resulted in a series of lengthy hospitalizations, crushing family circumstances, serious, intermittent contemplation of suicide, and nearly lifelong epic alcoholism. If anything, this is a biography of the man's soul.

The book is written in extraordinary but always compulsively readable detail. As seen in the endnotes, every fact or impression Blunk even hints at is drawn from Wright's extensively preserved journals, letters, drafts, and notebooks, as well as interviews Blunk carried out with seemingly every family member, friend, colleague, and poet who ever had significant contact with James Wright. Discussions and assessments of Wright's poems are themselves based largely on contemporaneous reviews, along with comments from the correspondence Wright maintained with the most important American poets of his era. This material is organized and presented so seamlessly that it reads with the engaging fluency of a good novel.

The *New York Times*, in its review, objects that the writing can be "desultory [and] full of fascinating but unintegrated information." But this misses the point that in following the paths of Wright's obsessions with poetry and alcohol, his financial struggles, and the ebb and flow of the relationships that mattered most to him, the resulting narrative is more compelling, brings us closer to the essence of who Wright was, and, most importantly, reveals more about the connection between the man and his poetry than would otherwise have been possible.

Despite being an authorized biography for which Blunk was given access to all of James Wright's papers, little or nothing is sanitized. Wright comes across as the least demanding person imaginable when poetry and alcohol aren't involved — but otherwise, all bets are off. When staying with friends, Wright habitually helped himself to every drop of alcohol he could find on the premises. He'd often wake up early, find a record in his host's collection whose music was important to his poetry, and spend the rest of the day blasting it at full volume. He spent a night in a drunk tank in Minneapolis following a barroom brawl, and at a series of literary events or parties, friends interceded to keep him out of fistfights. Otherwise, Wright was remarkably mild-mannered and courtly.

Perhaps most surprising to me was his transformation of a series of former female students into muse figures. With no physical relationship (despite his wishes to the contrary), Wright exchanged hundreds of letters with several young women, in which he mentored and encouraged them as writers, but also shared drafts of his poems and, in unsparing and yearning detail, his day-to-day moods, thoughts, and troubles. In casting these young women as muses, he often altered or transformed their personalities according to his needs, to the point of assigning names he invented for them. His perception and treatment of these relationships, each of which ended in heartbreak and worse for him, was often surprisingly mawkish, sentimental, and melodramatic. In one instance, he assumed without basis that the most important of these "muses" was dead; in other instances, he expected that some improbable twist would lead to a contrived happy ending.

These qualities finally led me to recognize why Wright was so fixated on Charles Dickens throughout his life, devoting his doctoral dissertation and significant amounts of his teaching to Dickens. I'm left with the impression that these were qualities of what William Blake would have called Wright's "Selfhood." It's a reflection on his ceaseless devotion to his craft that these impulses so rarely disturb his poetry.

At the very least this book is a must-read for anyone who might be seriously interested in writing poetry, or in seeing up close what it takes to write great poems.

A Review of

Marriage by Fire by Nancy Scott

BY ADELE KENNY

MARRIAGE BY FIRE
By Nancy Scott
Big Table Publishing
116 Pages
$15.00 Paperback

ISBN: 978-1-947896-01-7
To order: https://www.amazon.com/Marriage-Fire-Nancy-Scott/dp/1945917318/ref=sr_1_2?ie=UTF8&q id=1534719466&sr=8-2&keywords=marriage+by+fire

Nancy Scott has proven her "know-how" over the years as a skilled poet and as a collage and mixed media artist. Her newest book, *Marriage by Fire,* is a virtuoso blend of memoir-like vignettes and poetry that takes readers into the life of the fictional Claire—her divorce, passions, confusions, and her search for the one elusive soul mate who will bring her happiness.

Devastatingly down-to-earth, this book examines the life of a woman, mother, career caseworker, and a strong but essentially gentle soul. In the process of Claire's search for a loving relationship, as well as a search for herself, she weaves her way into and out of various lovers' beds. The conversations along the way are brilliantly written with dialogue that rings true and invites readers to stay with the story as they get to know Claire, the scarred, and the scoundrels.

Early in the book, "The Lady Was a Beard" (page 12) tells the story of a husband who preferred men.

I knew it before we were married.

… I thought I could outsmart it.
I buried it in the yard. It grew tentacles
and strangled the roots of trees.

That spring no buds appeared.
Neighbors feared a spreading blight.

… Those
who knew you were bewildered.
Some ladled platitudes; others said
you'd had a lapse in judgment.
The air grew weary with their words.
I hungered for the robust maples, poplar
leaves that shivered in the wind.
Anger gnawed on me with chiseled teeth.
I yelled at the barren trees. Neighbors
latched their shutters. I grabbed an axe
and hacked limb after limb
until the garden filled with splinters.

Claire's tale goes on to her role as a faculty wife ("Snapshot of an Ivy League
Faculty Wife," page 16):

My husband's chairman asks me to dance,
his arm brushing my breast, his fingers
weaving through my dark hair.
The sacrificial lamb, I keep smiling.
Oh how I keep smiling. And the band
won't stop playing fox-trots.

Although there is humor in the narrative and in the poems, this collection
addresses the lives of many women who sacrifice themselves in relationships that
fail in their search for emotional fulfillment. This is a collection that's very much
about why we do the things we do ("Mind If I Use Your Toothbrush, page 55):

    If I ever wanted to reach for real intimacy, I would
    have to give Mike up for good, forget the way he touched
    me, moved in me, and made me respond. I wasn't sure I
    could do that.
       Mike went into the bathroom and called out, "Mind if I

use your toothbrush?"

"Help yourself," I replied.

In "Upstairs at Edgmere," Claire becomes involved with Andy, a public figure. Sample this fragment (pages 77 and 80):

> For the next half-hour, we drove in wrenching silence, punctuated only by Andy leaning on the horn several times and complaining, "Damn, why can't that sonofabitch stay in his own lane?" then he offered, "I have a half-finished proposal waiting for me and I have to clean up the house. I haven't touched it for a week." He reached over and took my hand. "I'm sorry, Claire. I don't want to burden you with this."
>
> "It's not a burden," I said. "Don't overthink it."
>
> I had glimpsed Andy's moodiness from time to time, though he carefully kept it out of his public life. Andy was always the guy with the big smile and hearty handshake. Trying to cajole him into a better mood was a challenge I wasn't up for.
>
> Andy and I remained friends. He got divorced the following year. When a political shake-up took him out of the running for a senate seat during the next election cycle, he decided to start over in Arizona, where I understand he's been very successful. Good for him.
>
> Ben and I finally got divorced after months of wrangling in court. it was probably fitting that we were married on my birthday and divorced on Bastille Day.

The poem "Easter Week" (page 81) that follows describes a meeting with an old friend named Kate who apparently had a "crush" on Andy but was married to someone else and was jealous of Andy's relationship with Claire. Claire humorously notes that Kate should get her eyelids done and surely dyes her hair. When Kate says, "Andy married a bitch," Claire says, "I wouldn't know." She's looking at her watch, her coffee cup is empty, and there are tulips wilting in her car. Clearly, Claire is finished with that episode in her life, and the "write off" is expressed with a strong sense of authenticity in the subtle humor that speaks to human emotion and reaction.

This is a book about discovering who we are and how we learn to tell the difference between what we want and what we need. Claire takes life head on with kinetic fervor, as well as with vulnerability. The reader wants her to succeed. Although there are moments in Claire's story that are a kind of Tom Jones frolic, they are distinguished by layers of deeper meaning. Aside from the obvious skill with which the book was written, what stands out most is the main character's fierceness and her refusal to give up despite the knotty world of complicated relationships, confusion, and disappointment. Superbly written and delightfully engaging, this book is gutsy, sexy, and poignant all at the same time.

POETRY

What We Keep

Joe Weil

(For Adele)

I kept a lipstick stained cigarette butt
from my mother's fancy ashtray
for ten years, transferring it from pants to pants,
to roam among my ticket stubs and rosaries—
a free ranging reminder, not of what killed her
(yes, it killed her) but of my Ma in high spirits,
a whiskey sour in her left hand, a Chesterfield in
her right, gesturing to "company," making the room
laugh, her slender arms moving to the rhythms of her
wit. She was a "howl" as they said back then.
Though I knew the other Clare, who stared out the
morning window at a dark sky, her first son
brain damaged, him, constantly rocking
in his hospital bed upstairs, him breaking the plaster walls
with fists relentlessly pounding,
him, breaking her nose when she tried to change his diaper.
I knew a hundred Clares, all funny, all stressed,
all smoking two packs a day—my childhood
a swirl of blue smoke and bobby pins,
and my brother's monthly ambulance rides.
His heart stopped forty times, and on the fortieth
she still made sure she folded our laundry, paid the bills,
over cooked the roast.
She died at fifty, a three inch hole in her face.
Her green eyes closed by a tumor that
grew in the middle of her forehead. I kept that cigarette,
not as a cautionary tale, not as some gavel to hammer down

on the damage of her addiction—but because
I loved her, because it was nothing the world
would ever value, and that meant it was mine.
And when I finally lost it, or rather, made the mistake
of going to a dry cleaners, it was as if she'd died
again. I held those stupid pants for a long time
pulling out their pockets, absurd, lost, sniffing
for her scent.

NONFICTION

Up From the Killing Fields: Cambodia

Esther Whitman Johnson

Up all night on a bench in the freezing terminal of the new Bangkok airport, my teeth chattered, my back ached, my butt was sore. I fumed, in a foul mood. Construction clamored twenty-four/seven as crews built fast food stalls, boutiques, and restaurants in what seemed The Mall of the World.

Having crossed the International Date Line, I sank fast into the Blur Zone. Was it yesterday or tomorrow? Desperate for sleep, I pulled my backpack on and wandered bleary-eyed through the terminal, watching an army of night workers restock shops in every direction.

I'd fallen in love with Asia six years earlier teaching in China, and doing a Habitat build in Cambodia was a great way to get back to the continent. Getting to Cambodia, however, was proving more difficult that I'd expected—way more difficult.

It was time to check on my missing luggage. Again. Lost since the night before when I arrived in Hong Kong, my bag was evidently on an adventure of its own. "The Chinese are good at many things," said the weary Sudanese in the lost luggage line, "but service is not one of them. They smile and say everything will be fine, but it never is."

The airline rep *Yes, Madamed* me to death, a smile frozen on his face. "Not to worry, Madam, your bag fine." The bag was *not fine* in Hong Kong the night before, *not fine* in Bangkok that day, and would *not be fine* in Cambodia either.

When I arrived in Phnom Penh, my luggage was in Dubai. Thai Air blamed Air Emirates, which blamed United, which blamed Thai Air. No one took responsibility, and no one offered to deliver the bag upon its return from the United Arab Emirates. At *Lost Luggage*, the Cambodian official told me to return the next day. "Possibly it be here. Or not."

*

"I take you to city, to hotel, three dollah, verrry cheeep." A sing-song voice followed me out of the airport, continuing as I stood in line at *Money Exchange*. Three dollars was cheap. My guidebook quoted seven dollars for a taxi into Phnom Penh, so I looked up to investigate the driver.

Forget the luggage, just get into town. Lost luggage had liberated me on trips before, so why wouldn't it now? I followed Verrry Cheeep from the terminal into the parking lot, looking for his taxi. Instead he led me to a dilapidated motorcycle, picked up his helmet, grabbed my backpack, and indicated I should sit behind him.

"No way. I'm not getting on a motorcycle behind someone I don't know in a city I don't know. Besides, I have no helmet." My father's surgeon voice echoed in my head, the voice that repeatedly told his children during dinner what he had operated on that day, what had been scraped from the road after motorcycle accidents.

Verrry Cheeep took off his helmet and handed it to me. "Here, Madam, you wear. Verrry safe. I good driver. My name Hount."

What a ride. The perfect sail into Phnom Penh, a seedy, old French-colonial city. Clutching Hount's shirt, I stuck my chin into the breeze, the too-large helmet flopping on my head. Phnom Penh, what I imagined Saigon might have looked like before the French departed and all hell broke loose. The sweetness was doubled by nostalgia for China, where I had last ridden a motorcycle, hanging onto the waist of one of my beloved students. I could feel myself back in Taiyuan, roaring through the night streets. I had fallen in love with China. Cambodia could be my next Asian affair.

*

Dropping my pack at the hotel, still without sleep, I hopped back on the motorcycle to ride fifteen kilometers of dirt road into the countryside to the infamous Killing Fields. "Madam, you want I stop here?" Hount called back to me, pulling off the road. "You shoot live chicken with AK 47. Verrry cheeep, only five dollah. Many tourist do. Killing Field just down road. We almost there. You shoot chicken now. I wait."

"No thank you, Hount. I don't shoot chickens."

Hount kickstarted the motorcycle again, and I chewed dust, hanging onto his waist as we sped a few hundred feet further to the site. A three-dollar ticket at the information center, a stick of incense, a brief walk through a former orchard, and I was there. But nothing had prepared me for the Killing Fields—not my guide book, not the movie, not Hount's broken-English monologue. Nothing. I stopped cold at the stupa. Large skulls, medium skulls, baby skulls—eight thousand bleached skulls—side by side, filled glass shelves floor to ceiling, cases rising on all four sides of the stupa. Eight thousand skulls dedicated to the memory of three million people who lost their lives during the brutal Khmer Rouge regime.

I read the explanation—no, not an *explanation*, who could explain such a thing? I read the *history* three times, trying to understand:

Tiferet

*CHOEUNG EK GENOCIDAL CENTER
HELL ON EARTH IN 20TH CENTURY
PHNOM PENH KINGDOM OF CAMBODIA*

Established in 1975 by the ultra-communist Khmer Rouge, in two years the "security center" oversaw the murder of twenty-thousand victims, whose mass graves covered two hectares of land—*diplomats, foreigners, intellectuals, officers, soldiers, workers,* said the pamphlet. When Cambodia was liberated by the North Vietnamese, 129 mass graves were found, 86 excavated, and 8,985 corpses exhumed. Built in 1989, the stupa in front of me was dedicated *as a symbol of the cruel and barbaric homicides committed by the Khmer Rouge Communist Regime.*

Stunned, I could not speak and was glad to be alone. I've never been to a Nazi concentration camp, but I imagined it might be similar, a hell hole of inhumanity masquerading as a peaceful country orchard. Birds fluttered in the surreal quiet, and the sun shone on large depressions of shallow mass graves. Looking at the skulls, unable to avert my eyes, I remembered the most horrifying film I'd ever seen and committed myself to watching *The Killing Fields* again when I got home.

I returned to the motorcycle, shaken; surely Hount recognized the look of shock, having seen it many times. He said nothing as we passed the chicken-killing range, and we exchanged not a word on the ride back into Phnom Penh.

Early the next morning, I woke, went up to my hotel's rooftop terrace, and looked out at the convergence of the Tonle Sap and Mekong rivers. Alone in the open-air restaurant, I watched as the river below awakened—fishermen, houseboats, tugboats, barges. The sun struggled up through dusky clouds, streaking the water, bathing everything in golden light. Flags whipped metallic poles, tinny music floated from boats, a sultry breeze lifted the tablecloth, and the smell of charcoal assaulted my nostrils. Early risers practiced Tai Chi at a red pagoda across the street, while I sat at a table in the sun, eating a cheese omelet, drinking strong coffee, and shooing away birds fighting for crumbs.

I'd have no time to visit temples after the Habitat team arrived, so I hurried across the street, past beggars and vendors, into a calm courtyard of manicured bushes, potted palms, bursting azaleas, and a dazzling pagoda. A shimmering gold roof swept upward, cranes extending from each end. A stone elephant peeked through foliage, its body hidden by yellow mums. A silver dragon reared its head, pointing its fish-like snout into the air at proud lions who bared their teeth, guarding a door. I was tripping through fairyland.

Could I be in the same city as the Killing Fields? In just twenty-four hours there, I understood my guidebook's characterization: *Phnom Penh is at times beguiling, at times chaotic and charmless.* A scenic riverfront, fabulous food, cheap beer, good massages, architectural gems, and a diamond-encrusted golden Buddha—enchanting. Yet children and limbless people begged on every corner, poverty-stricken families lived in squalid boats on the river, and motorcycle traffic was not only an eyesore, but life-threatening.

A few days later, I went back to the Killing Fields with the Habitat team in the van. Why? Once should've been enough for any sane person, but the team was going with Leak, our local Habitat representative. She would tell her own story, and I wanted to hear it.

"During the terror of the Khmer Rouge," Leak said, "almost the entire population of Phnom Penh poured into the countryside. My mother told me of leaving home on a forced march of many miles. The city became a ghost town. You might wonder how a small group such as the Khmer Rouge could move an entire city's population and keep it from coming back. They were not stupid, the Khmer Rouge. They ran through the streets telling the people, 'President Nixon is going to bomb the city.' Everyone believed it, because the U.S. had bombed elsewhere in Cambodia, expanding the war in Vietnam across the border into our country. Why wouldn't people believe that Phnom Penh was next? Seemed logical. The Khmer Rouge told families to grab a few things and flee into the countryside. Once they got everyone out, they threw up roadblocks and would not let the residents come back."

Some of the team members shuffled in their seats, uncomfortable when American military action came up. But Leaf continued the tale, seemingly unaware of the tension in the van. "Then came genocide. The Khmer Rouge could arrest you for any reason. Intellectuals particularly were targeted. Wearing eyeglasses could get you killed, because glasses suggested you could read, and reading meant you were an intellectual, therefore an *enemy of the people.*"

A couple of the team members looked at their watches, maybe wondering how long they would have to listen to the story, but Leak wasn't finished. "When you go to the museum, look at the photographs the Khmer Rouge took of their victims—and they kept good records, took photographs of every single one—all the women have short hair. The Khmer Rouge made every woman cut her hair. Now, look around Cambodia, and you will not see a woman with short hair. Everyone remembers and associates short hair with that horrible time." Leak was right. Not once in Cambodia did I see a woman with short hair. Regardless of age, they wore long hair, mostly pulled back in a ponytail.

Tiferet

Leak pointed to my clothes—black pants, black shirt, what I always wore traveling. "You'll never see a Cambodian today, man or woman, dressed in all black. It's what the Khmer Rouge wore, even black head scarves, and the memory of that hated group is strong. You may see someone in black pants or shirt, never both. We will not dress like that again. Ever."

The rest of the team was as stunned by The Killing Fields as I'd been. On the way back to our hotel, the youngest member of the team—just twenty-six—wondered aloud. "How come they didn't teach this in school? We learned about the Holocaust. Why not this?"

Too quickly, I replied, "Maybe the same reason I grew up knowing nothing about Japanese-Americans in internment camps during WWII." I was lecturing, but I couldn't help myself. "Maybe because we Westerners place a higher value on white Europeans than Asians and Africans. We intervene in Bosnia but not Rwanda, study the Holocaust but not the Killing Fields." It wasn't that simple, I knew, but I was on a rant fueled by the second visit to hell.

No one responded.

Twice to the Killing Fields should have been enough. Yet a couple of days later I visited another of the hellholes of Phnom Penh—Tuol Sleng, a former Khmer Rouge prison, originally a high school. A high school—how depraved can people get? Take a place of learning and turn it into an interrogation center and prison. Take fourteen classrooms, divide them into cells, holding twenty to thirty prisoners each, legs shackled to an iron bar down the middle. Do not allow prisoners to move without permission. If a person defecates without asking, beat him with twenty to sixty whip lashes.

Deathly quiet. No one spoke in Tuol Sleng, although numerous visitors wandered through the building. In rooms where victims had once been brutally beaten, large black and white photographs of dead, battered bodies hung on the walls—photographs taken by the Khmer Rouge. Metal beds, leg irons still attached, stood as reminders of the horror. Sun poured through dingy windows onto tile floors, stained red, where blood once flowed during hours of torture.

"I cannot take any more death on this trip," I said as I left. "I am finished with it."

Only half the Habitat team had visited the prison. The rest had gone ahead to a restaurant for our evening of Khmer traditional dance and were in high spirits when the rest of us staggered in. One of the guys challenged another to eat embryonic duck eggs, a local gourmet treat. He hacked off the top quarter of the shell, found a partially-formed baby duck in a viscous film, swigged it down, little duck and all. No one stopped half-way; it was all or nothing. I joined the beer drinkers rather than the duck swallowers.

After the duck drinks, a group of AIDS orphans performed traditional dances. Teenagers garbed in native silks, faces painted like Khmer masks, contorted their hands and feet in ninety-degree angles, writhing to bewitching reed music. Tiny barefooted children, future dancers, peeked from behind bamboo screens at their adored older siblings. Sponsored by the government, the teens were in great demand and had even performed for the king. During their dances, I was finally able to let go of skulls from the Killing Fields, let go of blood from the school prison. Those beautiful teenagers, proud and professional, represented Cambodia's future, and that was where I needed to look next.

But not everything the Cambodian government did was as well-received as the AIDS orphan program, and we learned early on that our Habitat build was fraught with controversy. In downtown Phnom Penh, not far from expensive real estate—such as the Hotel Le Royal, a famous watering hole of rowdy foreign journalists covering the Vietnam War—an ugly squatters' town marred the landscape. Newly renovated, the hotel had become upscale, and the neighborhood was changing fast.

"Squatters must go," the government said, "like it or not." They were being evicted, sometimes by force, relocated to the countryside outside Phnom Penh, and given a small plot of land. Far from jobs, relatives, shopping, medical and other services, the countryside was not a popular option. Depending on traffic, it took forty-five minutes for our Habitat team to drive to the build, and we drove directly there in our own van. It would take considerably longer for the project residents, most of whom had no transport, to get to and from downtown. The round trip could easily eat up a day. So some families, refusing to live in the country, sneaked back into the squatters' town, evicted again and again. What was the government to do? In order to move into the ranks of its more-industrialized Asian neighbors, Cambodia had to eliminate urban blight and renovate. A plot of land in the countryside seemed a good trade-off for a poor family living in urban slums, but not everything could be measured in monetary terms.

One day on the way to our rural building site, Leak—ever the guide—took us on a detour at the outskirts of the city. "I want to show you something, so you understand *real poverty in* Cambodia. The people in the Habitat community where we build are the *working poor* with income, little as it is. Today you will see the worst poverty, homeless people who have absolutely nothing. Hundreds of people scavenge in the city dump every day, looking for food and anything they can use or sell—plastic bottles, old tires, metal pieces, paper, anything."

Would I have taken visitors to see the underbelly of my city? Probably not, but I admired Leak for having the guts to do it.

The road led us into what could only be described as Hell, an inferno straight out of Hieronymus Bosch. A smoky haze hung over the place, obscuring the sun. Acres of trash surrounded the road on both sides as far as I could see. Tiny, barefoot children, no older than two or three, sifted through rubble, dragging sacks behind them, searching for anything of value to take to their parents. Families lived—no, they didn't *live,* they *existed*—under plastic tarps pitched inside the dump. Worse than the slums of Lima, the most awful I had ever seen, this was the depths of human degradation. I should've taken photos to record the abject despair, but I couldn't lift my camera and didn't want to be a crass foreigner. It mattered not; that scene is indelibly printed in my mind.

"I show you this," said Leak, "as a point of reference for the community where you will build. Our homeowner, Vien, is a motorcycle mechanic with a business in his home, making the equivalent of ten U.S. dollars a month. He will live in the new house with his twelve-year-old son, Vauth. The mother died a couple of years ago, from typhoid fever, I think. You will think Vien is poor, but his poverty is nothing like this."

Vien had torn down the tin shack where he and Vauth lived, pushing their belongings into a corner of the lot while we built the new house. Their temporary bedroom was a double bed shaded by a sheet tied to trees; everything Vien owned was exposed to the weather, but it was dry season, so he wasn't worried. A photograph I took of all Vien's worldly belongings shows a few clothes, a tiny gas stove, dresser, small wooden chair, and mechanic's tools. You didn't want much when you lived without locks. Why buy stuff so others could steal it? A simple thing, a door with a lock, would make all the difference in life. When we left, Vien would have a sturdy one-room block house—three windows, a concrete floor, two doors. And keys.

By the third day of the build, I'd lost my heart to tiny, motherless Vauth. Twelve years old, he didn't look a day over eight. At first I wondered why he was only in third grade because he seemed intelligent. But since Vien needed his son to help him in the moto repair business, Vauth went to school only sporadically and had lost years of education.

Every day during break, I pulled out my flash cards and puzzles and worked with Vauth, told him it was a game, that we were playing school. "What's two plus two?" I asked in English, holding up the cards with numbers, and Vauth responded with fingers from both hands. His responses were quick and enthusiastic, his giggle infectious, as he squealed with delight at his right answers.

A couple of the team guys built Vauth a toy guitar from scrap plywood, and he played it like a pro musician, keeping the beat while our iPod blasted American pop tunes. Every afternoon we played soccer with Vauth and his neighborhood buddies, and by the end of the first week, we'd spoiled him as if he were one of our own kids. By the end of the second week, I dreaded leaving, knowing I'd grown too attached and would be ridiculously emotional.

And then it was time to say good-bye.

On the last day of our build, after the house dedication, we abducted little Vauth. "He's never been on a bus in his life," someone said, "and he may never have the chance again. Let's take him with us in the van for the farewell lunch. His father can follow on his motorcycle." We were not supposed to take Vauth with us in our vehicle—liability, of course—but we did it anyway.

Vauth was like a small child at Christmas, wide-eyed and thrilled. Not only had he never been in a bus, he'd never been in a restaurant. Scrubbed, clad in a plaid cotton shirt and khaki shorts, wearing flip flops on his rarely-shod feet, Vauth sat next to me in the restaurant. Like a preschooler, he played with the carved vegetable table decorations. Carefully, he placed a carrot flower on the head of a potato hen, creating a hat for her. In his hand, the hen strutted across the table to say *hello*. How different twelve-year-old Vauth was from the jaded American preteens I knew; there was nothing he couldn't imagine as a toy.

I have never felt on any other Habitat build the way I felt about that child, and I have met and interacted with hundreds of kids around the world. Knowing the boy just a couple of weeks, how could I have cared so much? Perhaps it was the dead mother thing, I don't know.

Near the end of lunch, I excused myself to the Ladies' Room. The goodbyes came next on the agenda, and I wanted no part of them. From the Ladies' Room, I crept outside and into the bus, where I pretended to nap to avoid a wrenching farewell with my little friend. Everyone hugged him in the parking lot—everyone except me—and Vauth hopped on the motorcycle behind his father and waved, a brave grin on his face. But as they pulled out, tears streamed down his brown cheeks.

Twenty-four hours later, in a Hong-Kong stop-over, I stood with thousands of spectators, watching the Chinese New Year's parade—hundreds of elaborate floats, bands, Lion and Dragon dancers, acrobats, musicians, soldiers, dignitaries. I should've been wowed, impressed by the parade and the lights in the harbor, *the most spectacular light and sound show in the world.*

Tiferet

But all I could think about was a child in a village in Cambodia who would likely never see such a parade in his life. A child who took delight in something as simple as a carrot and radish-top toy.

NONFICTION

Of Prophecy and Dream

Shara McCallum

> *The same one they sold into Egypt*
> *is the same one free them.*
> *I say the same one they sold into Egypt*
> *is the same one free them.*
> *The same one they sold into Egypt*
> *is the same one free them.*
> *Wo-yo-yo. Wo-yo-yo.*
> *What a ting, Selassie, what a ting.*

This verse is what remains in memory of a hymn I sang in childhood, at a time when I was possessed of or was possessed by a great faith. As a young girl in Kingston in the 1970s, I was raised as a member of the Twelve Tribes of Israel, the Rastafarian group to which my family belonged. While I have lived outside of this community for over thirty years and no longer practice or adhere to the belief system, lessons it imparted early on indelibly shaped me and I have carried them, as with this hymn, with me since.

The refrain—*the same one they sold into Egypt is the same one free them*—contains the whole of the story of Joseph, a tale of jealousy and its consequences, of one's ability to endure and overcome slavery and exile, of the power of prophecy and dream. Originating in the Torah, Joseph's narrative was later incorporated into and retold in The Old Testament and the Qu'ran. Rastafari's 20th century adoption of this Jewish account replicates what humans have done for thousands of years—borrowed from (or often usurped) the myths of other peoples to reconstitute those as part of a new set of beliefs. With each telling of Joseph's saga, in a changed social, political, spiritual, and temporal context, Joseph has been transformed to suit the needs of the developing faith.

Who Joseph *becomes*, in the context of Twelve Tribes in the 1970s in Jamaica, is replete in the hymn's summary of his story and implicit commentary on it. Joseph was one of the youngest sons of the Jewish patriarch Jacob (who would later become *Israel*) and the most beloved of his father's children. Sibling rivalry is a leitmotif in the Torah, and Jacob's preference for Joseph spawns jealousy in his brothers, who in turn plot to kill him. Persuaded against doing so by their youngest brother, they throw Joseph into a pit before selling him to a passing caravan of slavers. Ultimately he lands in Egypt and, through a series of further dramatic events, rises to become Vizier, second only in power to the Pharoah himself. It is in Egypt, in exile, that Joseph goes from being the one who was betrayed to the one who saves, from slave to prophet and interpreter of dreams.

It makes perfect sense to me now, as it didn't occur when I was a child singing without the fullness of understanding, that Joseph's narrative would assume a central place in Rastafarian culture and be codified in one of our hymns. In Twelve Tribes we did not have a written text unique to our faith but developed liturgy by reading the Holy Bible and through song and prayer. Our leader Brother Gad instilled in us an understanding of scripture not only as parable, warning against human foible, but as akin to dream, containing signs for us to divine our present moment and foretell the future. Within my family, my mother read the bible aloud to me and my sisters, *a chapter a day,* explaining the stories we imbibed as allegories, written thousands and thousands of years ago to foreshadow our lives.

Joseph's story had forecasted our own experience as Jamaicans, people of largely African descent who had been sold into slavery and were now living in exile. Like Joseph, as Rastas we were charged with serving as prophets in a foreign land. And, as is often the case with prophets, we were at first neither heard nor heeded.

When Rastafari began to emerge in Jamaica in the 1930s and up until the latter part of the 20th century, Rastas were widely regarded as pariahs. They were viewed as degenerates and potentially dangerous—politically and existentially. Jamaica gained its independence from Britain in 1962, but the yoke of colonialism is not one thrown off in a singular moment or gesture. The Rastafari world view, imparted to me as a child, offered a path toward dismantling the pervading colonial world order. Not alone, but in parcel with other anti-colonialist and anti-racist movements that gathered force inside and outside of Jamaica throughout the 20th century, Rastafari as a movement helped to provide Jamaica with a different vision of ourselves as a people.

With this hymn of Joseph and others, my family and I and all our brethren and sistren in Twelve Tribes were prophesying this vision. In word and deed, we opposed the culture's worship of a system of economics that lacks moral compass, evidenced in the grotesquery of slavery. Staunchly anti-capitalist, we advocated for wealth redistribution as a way to work toward achieving social justice. Confronted by colonialism and racism, we rejected the premise of social hierarchy on which those systems are predicated and preached equality across class and racial lines (gender, I'm afraid, was somewhat of an oversight). Twelve Tribes included many mixed-race families like my own, but we recognized that it was the African in us that had been systematically denigrated and we looked toward the continent for self-worth, self-definition, and safe haven, the goal of repatriation being strong in Twelve Tribes when I was a child. Tuning our ear to the prophetic and messianic strains of Judaism and Christianity, we carried those into our present—identifying a contemporary African leader as the incarnation of God.

For Rastas in Twelve Tribes, Haile Selassie I, Regent of Ethiopia from 1916-1930 and Emperor from 1930-1974, was seen as an avatar of the divine—in the same way Jesus was and is believed by his followers to be the embodiment of God. In our greetings we affirmed this deeply held conviction: *I greet you in the name of His Imperial Majesty, H.I.M., who has been made known to us in the flesh in the form of Haile Selassie I, King of Kings, Lord of Lords, Conquering Lion of the Tribe of Judah.* I was three years old in 1975, the year Selassie died, yet throughout my childhood in Jamaica I called out to, praised, and celebrated HIM—*Jah, Rastafari, Selassie I*—as did all the members of my community

Prophecy and prophesying were pivotal to the fabric of the world I understood as a child, woven into such daily acts as this greeting and manifest in larger ways. In my memory, my family and community lived with a sense of impending Armageddon, which would be brought on by man's continued inhumanity to man and was especially present in the threat of nuclear war and devastation we feared would soon befall civilization. All this was foretold by the stories of the Jewish and Christian bibles, written down more than two-thousand years ago. Faced with these signs, like Joseph and other prophets of the biblical texts, we were to use words and reason to warn of the downfalls of the past and present and to *chant down Babylon*.

Though as a child I could not comprehend the fullness of the hymn's meaning, I think now it helped inculcate in me the belief that knowledge of suffering should lead us to something greater: to become like Joseph and to prophesy in another sense of that word. To speak of what we see, not only for our own benefit but also for the sake of others. It is a complex speech act we are asked to perform when we prophesy: one that registers our own pain—*wo-yo-yo, wo-yo-yo*, the lament in the hymn's response to the call of the refrain sounds this, the grief of exile and of being betrayed. But prophesying is also an act of speaking that conveys gratitude and wonderment—*what a ting*—at the gifts adversity and struggle can paradoxically instill in us: generosity, compassion, and a sense of our own power in the face of apparent powerlessness.

Tiferet

At the end of the story, when famine is upon the land, Joseph's brothers are forced to travel to Egypt seeking food. Standing before their brother, they do not recognize him and Joseph initially cannot bring himself to disclose his true identity, so ravaged is he twenty years later by grief. What a painful irony that the one who was forsaken by his brothers is the same one who would become their salvation. But what a marvel it is as well that the role Joseph is cast into is one he readily accepts and through which he understands and gleans a sense of greater purpose. *What a ting* that prophecy and dream have the power not only to deliver Joseph from enslavement and exile but to deliver his brothers who had betrayed him, to deliver the Egyptians who had enslaved him—all of them. *What a ting* indeed.

A Review of

The Infinite Doctrine of Water

BY ADELE KENNY

THE INFINITE DOCTRINE OF WATER
By Michael T. Young
Terrapin Books
96 Pages
$16.00 Paperback
ISBN: 978-1-947896-01-7
To order: https://www.amazon.com/Infinite-Doctrine-Water-Terrapin-Poetry/dp/1947896016/ref=sr_1_1?ie=UTF8&qid=1534426769&sr=8-1&keywords=the+infinite+doctrine+of+water

Michael T. Young's voice is a masterful blend of intelligence and skill. This poet's work demonstrates linguistic commitment to deeply felt experience. Most importantly, Young's work is infused with a profound spiritual sensibility that speaks to the mystical and to the Divine ("Surfacing," page 26):

Unanswered questions return
        with the regularity of the photographer's
golden time, the persistence of shadow
           lengthening toward the ideal moment,
which is so hard to believe in and yet,
        even the papers report the next day
how a man on a beach discovered
        a bag of unopened letters in the water,
all of them prayers addressed to God.

The poems in this collection are the products of attentiveness and reflection. Young offers his readers unexpected awarenesses that he finds on city streets and in the natural world. In the poem "Feeding the Chameleon," he writes, after feeding a cricket to a chameleon (page 12):

Then I watch the Hudson pass in its flashing brown skirts.
I hum a bit of a Prokofiev sonata, scratch a note

about tourists snapping shots of themselves,
this need to say *I'm here.*
I scratch at the paint on the bench, scratch
at every surface until I find something
for which I won't ask to be forgiven.

Throughout the collection, the reader encounters transformation and the power
of revision that leads to self-realization and openness of the self within the larger
world. In "Reading for Pleasure" (page 24):

… as when we reclined on a beach at midnight
and one flash of bioluminescence hyphenated the breakers
making the dark into a thick scribble of text, where an aqueous
editor tested the buoyancy of each rewrite, and we sat back,
silent the rest of the night, watching for the next revision,
mindless of the final version and who, in the end, would own it.

Although Young's work is powerfully spiritual, it's never self-consciously
religious and it doesn't stand on superficial pretension. It's spiritual, not because
it mentions God, but because it affirms God's presence in the poet's life, the
poet's involvement in God's created world and, in a more collective context,
how humanity longs for communion with the sacred. Young approaches holiness
through the here and now ("The Generosity of the Past," page 28).

If time allowed us to forgive, that's mercy.
And I recall with every glass of wine
because it's who I am and what I knew
and I'm thankful for the generosity
of that time, for its store of meaning and thought,
which are to me here and now a kind of light:

for it's a light that makes a spectrum of mercy,
colorful thoughts as deep and rich as wine,
a generosity that's always new.

Forgiveness, mercy, and gratitude are leitmotifs in Young's work as he celebrates
life with a deep sense of wonder and humility. He creates moments in his poems
that are radiant with meaning as he examines his place in the world. In all of

these poems, Young builds brilliantly and gracefully on spiritual transformation ("Devotional," page 45):

At times the soul needs to crouch in its
cramped corners and scoop dust into piles,
feeling warm as a hamster under its woodchips.

At others, it needs to cut loose, divorce
itself from the intimate rooms of its sleep,
travel the long interstate toward damp fields,

… filling its lungs with its
crisp absence, its capacity to hold nothing back.

Young's is a meditative poetry that doesn't merely skim the surface of experiences, a poetry that avoids the obvious while reaching toward deeper truths, a poetry that incorporates stillness and awe as it reaches toward the unknowable and the holy ("Paperclip," page 66):

… that is, a wire
that's intoxicated, wandering in circles,
swiveling on its heels as it makes its way out
to meet friends that it embraces, holds together
in a maudlin circle of endearment,
all of which is also how I think of the infinite.

In this new collection, Young explores and situates what it means to be human. The poems are skillfully compressed and superbly crafted. Through the sonic qualities of language and its particular music, through use of caesuras (silences), through specific and extended metaphor, and through a deftly integrated whole of language, form, and meaning, this poet achieves for the reader exactly what the last lines of the last poem in this must-read collection express ("The Voice of Water," page 70):

Even after you've closed the book
it keeps reciting the lines.

Marcia Krause Bilyk   PHYSALIS

CARRIAGE HOUSE POETRY WINNER

Following are the 2018 winners of the Carriage House Poetry Prize, held biennially in conjunction with the Fanwood (NJ) Shade Tree Commission and Tiferet Journal. In observance of Arbor Day, the guidelines require that poems submitted contain reference to a tree or trees. This year's final judge was Donna Baier Stein.

THIRD PLACE WINNER

Japanese Cherry

Ray Cicetti

He never wanted (even as a boy) wings to fly like other boys, or like
a superhero to punch through walls when he could walk around
them. Once, he thought about being a star so he could shine each
night, but changed his mind, for what was the point of stars except
to see their light.

No, he always dreamt this is how it could be, to stand in a tree's
long journey. New growth around and through him, translucent
white blooms from every branch. Here, he catches the wind, knows
the rhythm of rain—head straight into the sky, feet rooted in the
earth. And he gives shade to those who need it, limbs for children
to climb.

Tiferet

This is the View

Susan Rothbard

It's still a surprise to see the moon
on a clear night even though you know
it belongs right where it is
above the evergreen you planted
when you first moved in, just to the left
of the birdfeeder you bought last summer
when you were trying to be like a woman
you admire who has a birdfeeder,
though you never expected you'd trudge
through snow to feed the birds which you fear
you've fooled into thinking it's okay
to stay through winter, and now you feel
this weight each afternoon when you come home
just before dark and the seed is gone,
and it's only after you've filled the tube
that you can take off your coat and read the mail.
Your devotion surprises you every day.
This is the view from the kitchen sink
where you scrub at the bottom of a pot
that won't let go of its stain, which is why
you draw in your breath when you see the moon,
even though it will always be the same moon.

CARRIAGE HOUSE POETRY WINNER

FIRST PLACE WINNER

Proverbs from the Owls

David Vincenti

for Elizabeth

In the woods, the only two choices are
quiet and danger. Seeing every direction
is easiest when winter emptiness fills
the forest. If you would hunt at night,
you must not waste even the smallest bit
of light. Majesty requires silence and,
after busy summer evenings, sleep.
Speed is found between the canopy and
the clouds, it will not join you in the nest.
To gain perspective, close one eye,
then the other. For wisdom, close both.

FICTION

Unconditional Love

Désirée Zamorano

When the phone rang Tuesday morning, Joan Samuels was halfway through her first cup of tea and morning ritual of counting the days. Two days until she made her weekly call to the lawyer's to see about her son Mark's appeal, three days until her weekly hair appointment, done just in time to visit her son, and four days before she was allowed to see her son again.

Tuesdays were interminable.

As the phone rang she weighed which outfit would be best. She enjoyed varying the pastel pantsuits she wore to the correctional facilities in an attempt to brighten her son's long days. But he would not be there forever, she told Mark, each week. Each week they were making progress on his appeal. Her son was not a murderer.

There was nothing alarming about the phone ringing at eight in the morning on a weekday. It could easily be her hair stylist, to move her appointment around, since Joan proved to be so English and so accommodating. Or it could be Naomi, one of the congregants from the temple she had recently joined here in Lancaster. But it wouldn't be Mark. This was not within his allowed hours.

"Joan Samuels speaking."

"Mrs. Samuels, this is Sergeant Frank Newhall calling from California State Prison here in Lancaster. There is no easy way to do this, so I need you to brace yourself." He paused for a few seconds. "Your son Mark Samuels passed away last night. There was no sign of violence, assault, or suicide. At the moment his death is being ruled as natural causes."

"I'm sorry?" Joan said. "Are you certain you are calling the right person? I just spoke to Mark two days ago, and he seemed perfectly fine. Perhaps you mean another Samuels."

"Mark Samuels, date of birth January 21st, currently forty-eight years old?"

Joan blinked. "Could you please say that again?" Before he repeated it, she hung up.

When the phone rang Joan backed away from it, as far as she could from its insistent ring. She staggered out of her small kitchen and into the hallway. The corridor was now never-ending, and without light or air. She knew by the weight on her chest that she had to keep moving, keep moving, keep moving though the dark hallway, but her legs, her arms were shaking, sinking.

She burst through the bathroom door. The sunlight burned her eyes. She would call her lawyers, she would call the prison. Some horrible, disgusting prank. Horrible, just horrible.

She sat on the floor and pressed a cold hand against her closed eyes. And if it were true?

That was when the strange sounds began, a crazed wailing. As if some poor creature watched while its heart was excised and shred before its disbelieving eyes. That poor creature, Joan thought, before realizing the wailing was her own.

She began to choke on her thoughts. Between the sobs something went the wrong way in her sinuses, which began to burn. She lay on the floor, setting her face against the cool tile, closed her eyes, and disappeared.

When she awoke she saw nothing but a white field of haze. She blinked and focused and saw nothing but white again. She was staring at the base of her toilet. She sat up and rubbed her cheek, where the tile flooring had left an imprint. The floor was filthy with grit — how could she not have noticed this before?

She went into the kitchen. Her telephone's red light was flashing, alerting her that she had a voicemail. She pulled a broom out from alongside the fridge, stepped back into the bathroom, and briskly swept it. She returned the broom to where it belonged, found her dustpan and disposed of the sweepings. From under the sink, she removed rubber gloves, a scrub brush, and cleanser. She went back into her bathroom, knelt at the wall farthest from the entrance, and began scrubbing . So much dirt and grit to loosen and remove. How appalling that she had allowed things to continue on in this manner!

It took her over an hour to clean the tile. She finished it all with a small toothbrush dipped in bleach going over the grout, again and again, and then a quick rinse of the floor with a damp washcloth. She put the cleaning supplies away with a sense of satisfaction.

She found her shower cap, tucked her hair underneath it, disrobed, tossed her clothing into the laundry hamper, and stepped into the shower. When she had showered, then dressed, in the lavender two-piece that Mark enjoyed so much, she checked her messages. It was Sergeant Frank Newhall again.

"How dare they," she said to the kitchen, shaking her head. "How dare they!"

Joan Samuels listened, took notes with her fingers trembling, and shook her head. His voice outpaced her hand, and she had to stop the message and start it all over again. His voice coldly told her she would need his birth certificate, her ID; she would need to make the arrangements with the mortuary of her choice; she would need to come in and officially claim the body; and she needed to do all this by the end of the day.

When she was done taking notes she hung up the receiver and wept. Her boy, her son, all alone. To die, all alone!

Wiping her face she went in her closet and pulled out an accordion file. Too much of dark London there to look at. She found Mark's birth certificate and placed it in her hand bag without glancing at it. Too many shadows.

She called Temple Beth Knesset. In Woodland Hills she would know who to call, but here in Lancaster? She left a message. She needed a recommendation for an undertaker to meet her at the facilities. She looked in the hallway mirror. No smearing mascara because she had not yet applied it. Her face needed a good dusting: blotches of red revealed to the world that she had been distressed. She took a deep breath and headed into her bathroom, now reeking of bleach and disinfectant mixed with soap and steam.

At sixty-nine years old, although the color of Joan Samuels's hair had changed, its style had not. It was a crisp, stiff flip that rose four inches off of her forehead, tapered down to her chin, then curled upwards at the shoulders. She ran her fingers through it, applied foundation, powder, then mascara on her lashes.

From London to Los Angeles to Lancaster. Her way of speaking was stiff and precise, which people she met assumed must be the English style for a woman of her class and breeding. Her London of forty years ago was cold, wet, and miserable. Mark's father was in and out of jail and Joan could never decide which was worse: his presence or his absence. The only sunshine, her son Mark. After all, it was her son who had given her the strength to call her sister Rachel, who had married and now lived in the States. With that call everything changed: she left Mark's father ("divorced" was the story she told; no one knew they had never been married, though today that wouldn't be much to hide—girls today would just as easily drop a baby as their knickers). She had brought eight-year-old Mark to her sister's in Woodland Hills. She found Daniel at the Temple, and, later, he asked her to marry him. What would he think today? What would he say?

It was hard to think of Daniel. For thirty-four years they had lived with each other. Each morning they awoke together; Daniel would blink at her, as if to himself, and say, "She's still here. She still hasn't come to her senses and left this funny looking Brooklyn Jew. Good morning, Goddess." Then he'd kiss her. Every morning.

That he should leave her, right after Mark's sentencing, six years ago. Death was unspeakably unfair. She blotted a mislaid dot of mascara.

Joan Samuels drove north on the freeway. Freeways made her nervous: the speed at which the cars streamed by, the impossibility of any civil communication, but she knew there was no way around it. Her hands gripped the steering wheel so tightly her knuckles were white and her fingers began to ache. The drive to the facility was ten minutes. Had she stayed in Woodland Hills, had she not sold her home and financed her son's appeal, the drive would have been hours.

How odd, how strange, that even as a child Mark's intelligence, Mark's humor, Mark's beauty provoked so many people. The president of the homeowner's association had taken her aside when Mark was only nine, and complained over something petty. What had it been? He had accused Mark of something, vandalism perhaps; she had now forgotten. But she did recall her outrage. The envy and jealousy of other people had trailed Mark from the very beginning.

Imagine that, even as a child. There was that incident in high school, which the principal could never, ever prove. There had been a vindictive, malicious, vile lying girl trying to destroy his life, an excuse to mar his college application, but Mark got into the University of Michigan just fine, thank you very much.

Then Mark decided to transfer back home in the middle of his sophomore year. He had been dismissed due to plagiarism. "I can't help it, mum," he had said, "if great minds think alike."

What had she done that he was persecuted so? Was she still being punished for ever having loved Mark's father? And for loving him, even more perversely, after she felt his fists against her? That she never told Daniel.

In the beginning of this nightmare she he had almost laughed at the charges. Her son was not a petty criminal. Her son would not need to murder a drug dealer in order to steal his merchandise, use his credit cards—outrageous, preposterous!

She stopped talking to her sister Rachel when Rachel implied Mark's gambling debts were responsible for Daniel's death. She broke off her friendships with Esther and Helen when they suggested that Mark might actually be guilty of the crime he was arrested for. And when the jury, a dusky group of jurors, found him guilty of murder, there it was again, the jealousy and envy Mark provoked in the less talented around him, now sentencing him to fifteen years to life.

Fifteen years. Life.

Cars continued to pass her. She scanned the horizon for the signs of something ominous embedded in the smog ahead, the billboards that lined the highway. Joan turned off of the highway and onto the road that led to the prison.

Tiferet

Almost fifty years ago in Middlesex hospital, Mark was born. For hours, for longer it seemed, they had kept him, so Joan was certain that there was something wrong with Mark, that he had been born with an extra limb or a missing one. But at last they brought him, and there he was: pink and squalling and desperate to suckle.

He had strands of white hair which would later turn dark brown. He had a snub nose, which pressed perfectly against her breast as he nursed. Nursing was more painful than the labor! But she persisted, releasing Mark only when he tilted his head back, stretching her nipple a ridiculous length.

Then there he was, fed and swaddled and sleeping.

Nobody had told her it would be like this. Oh, her mother, the doctors, her friends. All warned her about the pain of labor. The doctors discussed the mortality rate of mothers and infants. Illness, disease, brain damage. But no one, no one, had even hinted at the fact that across from her, in his hospital bassinet, was a little miracle, a perfect blessed miracle that had just emerged from her.

She explained this to the nurse who came in to take her temperature and check her pulse.

The nurse wiped Joan's forehead and said, "That's right, love, it is a miracle. It's a miracle that happens every single day. And because it happens to women, the world forgets what a sacrament it is. But we won't forget, will we, love? We won't forget."

The nurse bent over into the infant carrier, scooped Mark up, and handed him to Joan. The new mother closed her eyes and breathed in the bliss of the moment. No, she would never forget this. Ever.

Joan Samuels parked the car in the visitor's section of the prison. She unfastened her seat belt, stepped out of the car, and locked her doors. As she crossed the parking lot Joan thought about the infant she had nursed; the smile on his face when he returned home from elementary school; the smell of his neck as he leaned in to kiss her.

She entered the building to claim his body.

FICTION

Veiled

Rebecca Evans

Salome walks the market, the dust kicks beneath her feet. She is selecting veils. Her head, uncovered, depicts her marital status, unwed, and her nose jeweled with a single gold loop, her wealth, her beauty, and her availability. She chooses specific colors, they offer meaning. Oudem ensures flesh will win. Blue equals power. Green, immortality. Orange, fire, but for Salome this equates to passion. White, surrender. She needs seven. An important number, one of completeness and perfection. Tonight, she will dance before the king wearing only these seven veils.

This isn't how I see the scene. I see tonight as now. You humans measure time and if you're reading this, you are human. Humans write things. In my world, written word is unnecessary. We speak, and the idea is embedded within, like altering our DNA. We remember. Everything. No need for paper or pen or the binding of books. Contracts are sealed with thought alone and to articulate is to manifest into actuality.

Up here, nothing is bound. There is no human form wrapped in skin, just bundles of light. Except for those of us caught in between. We are unique entities on a singular mission. Me? I'm Baraqiel. I'm a guard. Right now, and now is all that exists, I am guardian to Rebekah. I'll explain in a minute.

And here, in my dwelling, all things happen at once. This is how Salome's shopping spree appears from where I sit. Unlike me, you see a specific time and location. You separate events and span them.

This isn't how it works.

You'll read this story in some ancient book, like the Bible or the Torah, and you'll believe that the king, Herod, is Salome's father. In your realm, it looks that way. So, you judge. *Incest*, you might say.

Let's pause here.

If time and space do not exist, and everyone and everything coexist in a simultaneous manner, then there are no fathers over daughters. Everyone is all things to one another and your current earthly spouse could very well be your mother.

Think about it.

Okay.

Maybe don't.

Keep it all veiled.

Tiferet

Let's move on with the story. It doesn't begin (an earth idea) with the market. It begins with a wager.

"Name your challenge," the Master spoke, the worlds quivered. The Collector of Debts smiled, a slow movement creeping over his face like the earth's long creek, as it was called later (another earth term) the Nile.

"The one garment, for all of time. If it goes out of style or out of use, the sisters perish. If it remains through all that expands before us, they live. Their children live."

"They meet?" asks the Master.

A sigh, which tends to feel like a warm south wind from somewhere in the Gulf where you live.

"Yes. They may meet."

The sisters, Rebekah and Salome, in your world, exist in the limited dimension of time, creating a barrier, one from the other. Hundreds of years, thousands of hours, as measured by humans, separate them.

"The garment?" asks the Master.

"A veil."

The Collector continues with the rules of the veil; it matters not if it is worn on the head or the toe, or the material of which it is made, it must be donned by only females—those who bear children—and it must hold them hostage on some level. If the veil ceases in style, he collects.

We watch the exchange. Gabriel, Cassiel, Eremiel, and I. The debt, we know, is the loss of everything. We won't whisper this to one another. No need. Our wings bristle against each other. Poor humans. So little understanding of time and space and the lack of distance between their actions and consequences. Their measurements off. Perceptions clouded.

They, or you, believe, all that is, occurs within confines of physical-ness.

I hate the Collector.

"Stop thinking," Cassiel warns me. "He will hear you and deny your mission."

We watch from above. Equal time. Their presence lived out in our time, current time. To them, they never meet. To us, they coexist.

It's complicated.

In your time, Rebekah lives first. I'm given the mission to convince her to wear the veil. If she fails to hear me, she loses the birth of her children, Esau and Jacob, and the written word will require altering, the future of her race will disintegrate, and Salome will never come into existence. That is in your world. I am desperate to get this right. She is ten and drawing water from a well and I've already spoken to Abraham, the father of Isaac, explaining the signs of his future daughter-in-law. Now I speak to Rebekah, I whisper, *I know water is precious, but satiate the camels of this servant. He will reward you.* Her youth offers less of a filter and she clearly hears me. She abides without hesitation. The plan works. The servant sees Rebekah as generous, offers her two gold bangles and a nose ring in exchange for her hand in marriage to his master, Abraham's son. Isaac. On this day, Isaac is 37 years old, considered aged, and you will reflect on this with some disgust that a man his age consummates his marriage with a mere girl.

Unacceptable in your time.

When Rebekah sees Isaac, a spiritual man, one who prays and retains a connection, I whisper again, *unworthy. Feel inadequate.* And she does. *Cover your shame. Seek a veil.* And she feels lack and on her wedding day, covers her face. In your time, centuries later, you see the beginnings of tradition; the bridal veil. You have no concept of the cost of this.

Should I have failed, my wings would singe and the Collector wins. As Rebekah's guardian, I take my mission seriously. We, up here, have only one mission each. One focus. Raphael heals. Michael fights *All The Time.* Gabriel and I, we guard. We are ones of many as you humans need much guardianship.

Here, as I said, yesterday is today and today is tomorrow and all that happens is happening concurrently, so while Rebekah marries and veils and feels shame, Salome continues her dance, which, to you, seems continents, and lifetimes away.

This is confusing. To you.

The Collector angers. The Master stills. We watch. We are careful with our thoughts. We work hard to protect the sisters, and we know the Master is pleased. This is our way.

Salome drops a third veil and Herod's manhood fills with blood, his face flushes, and he wants to take her. Her skin, like a sun-kissed olive, is flawless and goose-bumped with her own excitement. She feels power over men, her ankles draped with bells, jingle her cadence, her thrusting abdomen speeds in the desperate way of one who wants a man inside of her. One who gets what she wants. She wants Man. On a platter.

Centuries will pass, and women will striptease and wear bridal coverings, something they believe began with Rebekah and Salome.

This is untrue.

There is no start.

Tiferet

There is also no finish.

There is only now.

I've said it before. It seems complicated to you. I know. Stay with me. It gets easier.

Later (that human-earth term again), Rebekah and Salome cover themselves completely. Their names are different, and they are Muslim. Only their eyes peek through the khimar. They hold hands. They know each other now.

As they knew each other before.

In now-time, my time; a car accident, a sea parts, a tsunami hits, a flood, a man jumps from a bridge, and a woman gives birth on a bathroom floor. Time stands still. It really does. Humans cannot correlate this. China sits alongside America, which is next to Egypt, there are no separate continents. The pyramids are stars and the mountains are planets and the oceans are concrete floors. Somewhere.

The Master and the Collector play a game. Every so often. You'll recall Job, a different wager. A different story. Humans are like these game pieces to the Collector. Think of chess. A good game. We call it Life up here. The Collector presses on the circumstances, seeks a human response, he whispers, *kill*, and a nation destroys their own. *Burn*, and villagers set fire to one another.

But the Collector was unaware of the secret contract installed by the Master between the sisters. Long ago (yes, yes, your term), when Rebekah and Salome were only light, or source, or energy. They were entities without form, without human limitation. They sat up here, alongside us, side by side, agreeing to a pact. One to the other.

"We will meet," Rebekah says.

"We won't remember," Salome says.

"We need to wear the garment." Rebekah knows this, I've whispered it to her, remember? My words span all of time.

"I will," Salome says.

"Promise," Rebekah says.

"My word is a promise," Salome reminds her.

Then the Master pushes them through the gates, knowing their mission is critical, and on the way out of the great canal of birth, He presses his finger to each of their lips, leaving an imprint above their lip-lines. He tells them, each in their separate (as you perceive it, not us, up here) mother's wombs, "Shhhhhh. You must have courage. Forget all that you've learned. Remember who you are. Wear shame to protect your children. To protect your future."

The imprint rests on all who have traveled from this realm to your earth, to beat the Collector. To win the game.

You think there is an end in your journey. It doesn't cease.

We long for your return. We long for the sisters' return, but they must sort through the rules, wear the garment. Even more, they must define it for all of time, your time, so that those who follow will recognize the symbolic trend. If they accomplish this, they come back, two sources, two lights. Brothers-sisters-mothers-fathers. It matters not.

Salome drops a fourth veil.

Rebekah covers her face.

The sisters don a jilbab. Cloak themselves.

They feel unworthy. Believe themselves unworthy.

Time bleeds-speeds-slows-drops-stops.

The Collector seethes.

The floor is warm, like melded gold, and bejeweled. Light trickles through. The setting sun, deeply burnt, splashes colors across the room, towards the throne, where Herod Antipas watches, his belly round and full, his loins aching as Salome, clothed in a single cloth, is about to drop her last veil.

This is the room where Delilah severed Samson's hair, where Hannah bespoke a prayer for a son, where Sarai circumcised her husband without anesthesia, and where, after the dance, Herod will present Salome with John's head on a platter. Her payment, a debt collected, for revealing herself to the King, her step-father, and his guests. Salome learned the dance from Ishtar, the Babylonian goddess best known for her striptease-dance. Ishtar relinquished her robes at each of seven gates through the underworld in search of Tammuz. Stripping naked became a state of being, a state of truth, and the ultimate unveiling.

Salome slowly chuwls, hips pulsing, breasts gyrating in time to her movement. She wants the king to want her. She wants John's head. She longs for power. She hears a whisper, *remove the veil, but do not let it go.*

Gabriel speaks to her, *fake your weakness for you are not lesser than man.*

I, Baraqiel, whisper to Rebekah, *you are good, you are kind, wear the veil, only pretend to be less than man, teach your daughters.*

The Collector screams as Salome gains power over the king and Rebekah remembers she is good enough. And I, I did my one job. I did it well. And time, it does not move on. We stay here. We watch. There is no waiting (that is a human term), there is no waiting where I come from.

POETRY

Or What Did You Think I Do When I'm Doing Tai Chi?

Hedy Habra

Eyes set on hands
       flowing as an ink brush:
that's when my best strokes
          are continually rehearsed
over invisible rice paper. The air
      becomes dense, I move
as in a dry aquarium.
       Each gesture creates
          air waves pulling me back
      and forth as words
rearrange themselves,
         unfold effortlessly
on a constantly renewed
      board where signs and shapes
          merge and fall like autumn leaves
speaking within hidden folds.

POETRY

Or What If She'd Chosen to Drown in a River of Down?

Hedy Habra

Some want to drown in their dreams
or in amber drink, others in denial,
             whilst she thinks of a river
of clouds sweeping her high above, sinks

in a river of down suffocating—without
        wetting her auburn curls: yes, vanity
still prevails in such moments.

Is there something worth dying for,
she wonders? But maybe, just maybe,
        if you live long enough you may
cross the threshold of desire, its constantly

deferred lack, learn to yearn for sunshine,
                await the concert of birds.
Once upon the time, tempests took

hold of her heart. Chest tight, she withheld
her tears, realized she was never asked:
        "What do you really want?"
and removed the veil off her face.

There comes a time when ashes
        become so cold you can no longer
remember a fire was ever started.

There comes a time when you know
you've lost your moisture
                and if you dream of drowning
even drowning should be dry.

After *White (Ophelia)* by Joanna Smiélowska

POETRY

Boulevard Saint-Laurent

Julia Y. Knobloch

At the mountain's foot live lost Canadians, Jews and Portuguese,
they share distant horizons.

Blue and white tiles hibernate in a small park,
a sign in the sky reads Quincaillerie Açores.

My teacher lived in a sturdy house;
an involuntary prophet, a reluctant priest.

The city shows me how he turned reality into imagination.
The streets are all one song.

I am guided, even without his voice.
Royal equals holy here.

The Main combines bygone and enduring glory,
reveals the names of men I loved.

A taxi driver from the Kabyle mountains takes me to the cemetery.
He doesn't know I killed a Berber child.

Arctic winds blow around the shtiebel where I pray.
Ghosts from the future visit me before I fall asleep.

I took communion in my cousin's white lace dress,
in a church called Sankt Laurentius.

I walked far for water from graceful hands, mystery of sacredness.
A Jewish boy was curious about one and many saints in his native city.

The inconsistent things love makes us do are most coherent.

POETRY

Dear Lefty

Robert Rosenbloom

—for Max Joseph

We will wear the same outfits,
shirts with orange and yellow dinosaurs,
khaki shorts with bunched up elastic waist bands
held aloft by blue suspenders.
I need a store like Gap Kids for grandparents,
where I can buy t-shirts like yours
pocked with red and green footballs
flying end over end across goalposts.
All I need to know is your name is Lefty,
that you leaned on your mother's left side
during pregnancy, that you came from
her left-sided egg; that my pet-name for you
is D Train because the ambient noise
in your first ultrasound reminded me
of the subway line I took into the City,
its rhythmical *shshshing*
capable of rocking a baby and his newly minted
grandfather asleep.
One day we'll get lost and let ourselves
be pulled upwards by strong winds—
the ones city officials worry themselves sick over—
into Thanksgiving Day Parade floats,
up among trees and large balloons.
I will take your hand—
we will stand together as one.

NONFICTION

Pilgrimage

Cindy Carlson

> For in their hearts doth Nature stir them so,
> The people long on pilgrimage to go,
> And palmers to be seeking foreign strands,
> To distant shrines renowned in sundry lands.

Geoffrey Chaucer
The Canterbury Tales
translation from *The Art of Pilgrimage*

Despite the heat of the day, Rich and I were eager to complete our journey. We had endured the fifteen-hour flight that catapulted us a day into the future, followed by another six hours gripping the backseat armrests as our driver battled rickshaws, motorcycles and lumbering trucks through the maze of Mumbai and up over the rocky spine of the Ghats. This last hour would be on foot through the high dry fields of the Deccan Plateau.

We set out on the well-worn path under an immense cobalt blue sky with a friend who joined us like a spirit guide, the air sweet with grasses and wood smoke. A solitary herdsman in his white cotton *dhoti* squatted on his haunches in the shade of a neem tree. His goats grazed on sparse vegetation, oblivious to us passing by; every now and then one shook its head, sending a faint tinkling sound over the breeze. A bubbling chatter drifted from a utility wire above the path. I stared up at the drongo, India's version of the blackbird, recognizable by two extra-long tail feathers that curl at the tips like a handlebar moustache—the exotic cousin of the blackbirds in my marsh halfway around the world.

Farther along, the path divided—the right fork rambling a mile or two down the hill into the haze of the distant town. The left would take us to our destination.

I first encountered the notion of pilgrimage when I needed a classic literature class for my undergrad English degree. Chaucer sounded good—a bawdy tale of comic and compelling characters, long ago and far away. Then I read these lines:

> Whan that Aprill with his shoures soote
> The droghte of March hath perced to the roote,
> And bathed every veyne in swich licour,
> Of which vertu engendred is the flour,
>
> . . .
>
> So priketh hem Nature in hir corsages,
> Thanne longen folk to goon on pilgrimages
> And palmeres for to seken straunge strondes,
> To ferne hawles, kowthe in sondry londes.

Somehow—the lilting cadence, the arcane language, the story-telling—something about it stuck in my head. To the dismay of friends, I would repeat, "And smalle foweles maken melodye that slepen al the nyght with open ye" when I saw a bird. But mostly to myself I said, "Thanne longen folk to goon on pilgrimages." Over and over. It had seeped, inadvertently, into my soul.

I already knew I would be a traveler. The "licour" was in my "veynes." At that age I hadn't logged many miles to faraway places, but family excursions, birding trips, short jaunts with friends, a couple of wild spring break adventures and even a little hitch-hiking had already clinched my wanderlust.

Go, and then go some more.

This pilgrimage idea seemed different—an intentional journey often, as I understood it, on foot and with hardship, to discover something deeply meaningful. The thought was at once fascinating and frightening. I wondered what mattered enough to warrant so much effort. I wondered what mattered that much to me.

The "yellow car phenomenon" says that soon after someone mentions how many yellow cars he or she has seen lately, you will notice more yellow cars than you have ever seen in your life. It must work with talk about pilgrimage as well.

Soon after my Chaucer class, the pilgrimage idea started popping up in other places. My Jewish roommate wanted to travel to the Holy Land. The Sorbonne was drawing another, the French major. My sister dreamed of hiking the Appalachian Trail. They spoke of these places with such reverence I knew the pull wasn't about vacations. These women were seeking answers to deep questions about life, wanting to immerse themselves in experiences that offered a clue about how they would live it in the future.

So I started reading Jack Kerouac and dreamed of driving a red convertible across the country to San Francisco. I toyed with the idea of visiting Sweden, my ancestral homeland. I learned about the pilgrims of the Camino de Santiago hiking sometimes 800 miles to touch the relics of St. James. I marveled at stories of the "walkabouts" among the aborigines. These were beautiful fantasies, but none spurred a pilgrimage. There was something—time, money, fear, whatever—that always stayed my feet.

As if on cue, a dozen bee-eaters swarmed up from a stand of acacia trees, buzzing overhead, their dazzling green and blue feathers caught the sunlight like brilliant jewels. The birds looped along the left path as though leading us forward. We knew the way, but their company felt affirming.

The path was wide enough for the three of us to walk side by side. We'd hiked almost a mile—the sun warm on our backs, water bottles knocking in the pockets of our cargo pants—without seeing another soul; this trek would be made in the company of birds. They bee-lined toward an irrigated area and we followed. Giant pink and white hibiscus bloomed among the flowering trees of a small orchard. Our pace quickened. Up ahead through a row of banyan trees we caught sight of a brilliant white dome settled atop its small stone structure, decorated with symbols of the world's great religions, radiant in the sunlight.

On a November day, two years out of college, deep in conversation with new friends, I first heard the name of Meher Baba, the great Indian avatar and mystic. At that moment, I knew somehow my pilgrimage question had been answered. In a sudden, deep recognition, I knew he would become my spiritual teacher, and ultimately my pilgrimage would be to India—to his birthplace, his home, his ashram, and his tomb. The only question was when.

For a while, life got in the way of pilgrimage. There was work to be done and relationships to be undone. Then Rich and I married, and travel climbed to the top of our priority list. For the next twenty years, spurred on by our shared love of birding—as we wandered in Europe, Africa, the Far East, Central America and the Caribbean—we talked of India, but never made plans. It remained remote and unapproachable to me, veiled in a filmy mist, barely beyond my reach.

In *The Art of Pilgrimage: The Seeker's Guide to Making Travel Sacred*, author Phil Cousineau explains that "there are pulls a soul feels once or twice in a lifetime." It might be a call to renew a forgotten aspect of life or to rekindle a buried belief, or a desire to touch and experience a piece of history, or a longing to make an outward journey to discover an inner truth. You'll know the pull, he asserts, when you feel it.

We finally felt the pull in 2008, more like a whisper. Or a question. Rich was coming up on ten years in his post-retirement consulting business. Changes loomed in my job, and I questioned my energy to face them. Both of us were approaching milestone birthdays. We wondered: what do we want from our lives, and how do we choose to live them in the future?

Then the yellow cars arrived. It seemed as though everyone we talked to had just returned from India. There were glowing reports of a new, more comfortable, pilgrim center at the ashram in Meherabad. Flights to Mumbai were abundant; our frequent flier miles matched the amount we needed. And most compelling, the original residents, those fortunate ones who had known Meher Baba in his physical form, were all passing away. If their stories were to be part of our pilgrimage, we needed to go soon.

"India?" people asked when I shared my plans, in that way that made me wonder if I should have said anything at all. Reactions—likely based on *Slumdog Millionaire,* the popular movie set in the Mumbai slums, or *Eat, Pray, Love*, the New York Times best seller—ranged from "Why would you go there?" to "Why would you go on a pilgrimage?"

I laughed off the first question. Why not India? I'd never been there. And a pilgrimage? I tried to relate it to visiting Graceland, or re-tracing the Trail of Tears, or intending to set foot in all the minor league baseball parks.

"It's trying to touch what is most important to you," I said to a close friend.

"Then isn't all your travel a pilgrimage?" she asked. A fair question, but somehow this trip felt different.

Cousineau says, " . . . travelers cannot find deep meaning in their journey until they encounter what is truly sacred. What is sacred is what is worthy of our reverence, what evokes awe and wonder in the human heart, and what when completed transforms us utterly."

I discovered there was really no way to convey my expectations. Unlike pilgrims to the Blarney Stone, I wasn't planning to exchange a kiss for a blessing. Gurus and perfect masters claim that the grave site—or *samadi* in the local Indian dialect—of Meher Baba lies at the "om point," or the center of love on earth. Visitors there embark on a personal journey inward to recognize the divine within, and in everyone and everything. Each pilgrim's journey is different, but everyone comes away changed.

We dropped our sneakers along a green chain-link fence surrounding the tomb site; they looked suddenly new and opulent next to a few pairs of threadbare leather sandals. Stepping into a small covered courtyard, we were startled by a pair of ground squirrels skittering about the stone floor, tiny feet scratching in the stillness. A young woman with warm smiling eyes, in a sari the color of the sky, nodded her head in *namaste*, and as she gestured toward the tomb, her bangles softly clattered on her slender brown wrist.

I stopped at the doorway, suddenly seized with dread. What was I thinking to attempt this pilgrimage? What made me think I was worthy of this experience? Who was I to expect a connection to the divine? Or worse, what if I had come all this way and there was no experience at all?

Rich gestured for me to go in first. I stepped over the threshold, taking care not to step on it, as is the custom, and entered a twenty-foot square space—a cool, soft world, charged with a vibrant energy. From a window on each side, sunlight streamed in, almost enlivening the faces of the pale pastel frescoes that towered up the walls and across the domed ceiling. The tomb stretched before me, low to the ground, its gleaming white marble at the head exposed, the remainder draped in a heavy crimson cloth. And there in the center, fresh from that morning's devotions, rested hundreds of flowers—garlands of jasmine and tuberose, freesia, scattered golden asters, single red roses. The fragrance was overpowering.

I sank to my knees in wonderment. Resting my forehead softly on the nubby weave of the cloth, everything—fear, questions, doubt, worries, exhaustion, the chatter in my mind—everything dropped away. Only peace remained. Oneness. As though I was part of something ancient and sacred.

My pilgrimage was complete. I had arrived in that moment, both the ending and beginning of my journey.

POETRY

This is My Story to Tell

Michelle Aucoin Wait

This one of a mother, who silenced her daughters,
who loved something in or about a man
that allowed her not to fold her daughters
into her wings when he stormed. Her eyes
said, *the best girls know how to serve*
dinner in silence and go hungry for
affection when they over-salt the butter beans
or burn the cornbread.

This is my story to tell—this one that leaps to the tip
of memory when I see personalized leather
belts—names scrawled in country western
font always transform into his name
branded in dark leather then etched
in deep blues and purple across the backs
of my legs.

This story about the way I knew
to sit still and not cry so that the buckle
would not collide cold metal into my skin
or cause me to give him the satisfaction
of a solid tear.

This is my story to tell—this one
of a little girl that swallowed bile
with each bite as she sat in silence at the dinner
table, the girl who grew to hate dinner time
until she grew an egg inside her and hatched
out her very own duckling. *Child, imprint*
on me, but don't mimic my anxieties,
my neuroses, my ability to forgive

Tiferet

but never forget the way he would shame me
into submission,
silence,
the way she said at his funeral that he was a good man,
a good husband,
a good father.

This is my story to tell—the one of when
I buried her, I made sure only "wife," not "mother,"
was engraved on her stone.

POETRY

Grateful Conversations

Susan Rogers

Everything we have we're given
in love to use in love, in grace.
There is nothing we alone have written.

We are but a conversation
of light. Through this exchange we trace
everything we have. We're given

sour and sweet, lemon, raisin
and grain to bind them into place—
There is nothing we alone have written.

We eat cakes but have forgotten
their origin. We have erased
everything. We have; we're given.

We look. We laugh. We love. We listen.
We welcome gifts we embrace.
Yet there is nothing we alone have written.

Watch sunset turn to a ribbon.
Remember honey and its taste.
Everything we have we're given.
There is nothing we alone have written.

NONFICTION

Just As I Am

Andrew Hudgins

In the early sixties, I was standing in a Southern Baptist Church in San Bernardino, California, singing the altar call, "Just as I Am," when the preacher, as he'd done many times before, instructed the congregation to stop singing while the organist continued to churn through the tune and the choir hummed along. At the end of the aisle he stood with his head bowed, his right hand held high up, and over the wordless dirge, he called out, "God is talking to someone here today. I feel His presence. Won't you open your heart to Him? Won't you let Christ's sacrifice on the cross wash away your sins and save you from the torments of hell? Come now, come today; tomorrow may be too late." The preacher's voice chanting over the muted organ and the eerie humming of the choir was an otherworldly summoning.

Puberty's urges, which I'd been taught were dark urges, had left me feeling like my soul was, as the hymn proclaims, "one dark blot." Wretched with fear of burning eternally in hellfire, I was "tossed about/ with many a conflict, many a doubt,/Fightings within, and fears without." In tears, I looked at my father, and sobbed out, "I have to go down there." He nodded, and I staggered down the aisle, blubbering. "O Lamb of God, I come!"

I was thirteen, but Southern-Baptist Calvinism had already hammered its ferocious version of Platonism into me, not as a belief but as a marrow-deep understanding of the chasm between the ideal and the real, divine and mundane, soul and body—the purity of God and the depravity of man. *My* depravity. *My* worthlessness. *My* damnation. *My* inevitable descent into the flames of hell. The only possible way out of my predicament, which is everyone's predicament, was Jesus.

"Just As I Am" is as pure an expression of uncompromising Calvinism as has ever been set to music, and it is devastatingly effective as an altar call, a song designed to convince sinners of their sin and to offer the one and only palliative for their inherent wickedness. The song's imperative is to decide now, just as I am at this moment and "waiting not:"

Just as I am—without one plea,
But that Thy blood was shed for me,
And that Thou bidst me come to Thee,
--O Lamb of God, I come!

Just as I am—and waiting not
To rid my soul of one dark blot,
To Thee, whose blood can cleanse each spot,
--O Lamb of God, I come!

To that tune and those unsung words, I went.

The pastor presented me to the congregation as a newly saved soul, and asked for a show of hands as to whether I'd be welcomed into Christian fellowship. It was a ritual I'd seen dozens of times. No one had ever received even one negative vote or murmur of disapproval, but now that I was the one being voted on, I was perplexed at why democracy and human election had any role in dispensing God's grace. From the satisfied look on his sweat-drenched face, I was aware too that the preacher saw me as a trophy—a soul he had bagged for Jesus. He was presenting me to the congregation as proof of his effectiveness as a spiritual leader, yes, but also as a salesman who was good at his job, one who deserved to keep his job and who just maybe should get a raise at the end of the fiscal year. At that moment, he was both a prophet in the steps of Paul and Silas, and a successful huckster—and if the two identities were not the same, they were at least Venn-diagram circles with Set A (pure) and Set B (impure) sharing a lot of discomfiting overlap.

In church, I had stood singing this altar call, all seven verses, as many as five or six times as the sweating preacher kept us singing, humming, listening to the hushed organ—as he beseeched recalcitrant souls to abandon the pews and come forward for the free gift of salvation, and it was hard not to think of a desperate salesman wheedling: "What will it take to put you in the driver's seat of shiny new Eternal Life today? It might be gone tomorrow." Like like the smell of leather bucket seats and the rumble of an American V-8, the emotive oomph of "Just As I Am" boosts a sales pitch, though the hymn itself is not inherently manipulative. When Charlotte Elliot wrote it in 1835, she was, by her brother's account, working herself through a spiritual crisis, and she "set down in writing, for her own comfort, 'the formulae of her faith.' Hers was a heart which always tended to express its depths in verse. So in verse she restated to herself the Gospel of pardon, peace, and heaven." But in my childhood, the song was often used with cynical calculation for its effectiveness, and when the preacher flogged the congregation through many grinding, dispirited repetitions of "O Lamb of God, I come," I have, in a rage at being manipulated and a rage to go home and a rage to pee, prayed savagely that some wretched soul would walk the aisle so the preacher would shut the fuck up and let me quickstep to the bathroom and then out the back door to my car.

The morning I was saved, one other person came forward, a middle-aged woman. Her husband quietly joined her, and from the calm way they spoke to the preacher, I could tell she had already consulted with the preacher about joining the church. I felt superior to her because she must have made an intellectual decision about faith, while I had been struck by the Holy Spirit, convinced and convicted of my sin, like Paul on the road to Damascus. When I'd stumbled down the aisle, my lack of planning, my crying, my emotional agitation, and my terror were proof of my state of grace. Even if they were merely proof that I didn't want to spend eternity in Hell, I understood immediately that my sense of spiritual superiority had eradicated the spiritual grace to which I aspired. Or at least besmirched it. Though I'd been cleansed of sin by accepting God's grace, I hadn't been unsoiled long enough to feel unsoiled—three minutes at the most—before, with the sin of pride, I was already rebuilding my one dark blot. Or maybe I had screwed things up and never been cleaned. Either way, I knew that thinking my salvation was superior to someone else's was a particularly nasty bit of spiritual pride.

Salvation was going to be a fuckload harder than "Just As I Am" had taught me.

NONFICTION

You Are With Me, I Am With You: On Psalm 23, "Howl, Part III," and "Arrow & Bow"

Richard Chess

I am with you in Rockland

You are with me

I am with you in Rockland

You are with me

I am with you in Rockland

You are with me

You're madder than I am

You are with me

We are great writers on the same dreadful typewriter

You are with me

Where the faculties of the skull no longer admit the worms of the senses

You are with me

...in a straightjacket... losing the game of the actual pingpong of the abyss

I fear no harm

I'm with you in Rockland

You are with me

*

23. A David Psalm. Part III, "Howl," a Ginsberg poem.

I am not alone, sings the psalmist.

A thousand generations later, I am not alone, recites the mourner. Sandy Hook. Manchester. Paris. Orlando. Columbine. Baltimore. Chicago. Charleston. Her child gone. Her declaration, which she desperately wants to believe, to feel, to know in her heart, her bones, her soul, there in the sanctuary where the funeral for her boy proceeds, followed by the terrible daytime headlight crawl of a drive to the cemetery, the lowering of the plain pine coffin, the fist of the first shovelful of dirt striking the coffin's lid, the slow shovelful after shovelful of dirt filling the grave until

Tiferet

the hole in the earth is no more a hole, leaving only the hole in her heart.

My life He brings back. Robert Alter's translation. His comment on the verse: "Though 'He restoreth the my soul' is time-honored, the Hebrew *nefesh* does not mean 'soul' but 'life breath' or 'life.' The image is of someone who has almost stopped breathing and is revived, brought back to life" (Alter 78).

A mother, her child gone. She almost stopped breathing.

My life He brings back, she recites to ~~her~~self as she stirs honey into black tea, one mug on the counter on her first morning of living with her nearest dead. Maybe the psalm helps.

*

You are not alone, chants the poet, I am with you in Rockland, Rockland Psychiatric Center in Orangeburg, NY. Wherever I am when I call out to you, Lower Manhattan, Denver, Tangiers, I am with you, declares the poet.

*

But, really, how can that be when I am here and you are there, when we are separated by space, time, existence?

The distance: even an inch can seem like a mile, even a moment can seem like a light year. The exact moment when the distance between self and other, self and beloved, human and divine is felt most acutely—that's when the psalmist, the poet, declares: we are together.

A lyric impulse: to deny, to obliterate distance. To make the distance sing.

*

In the face of my foes. Psalm 23. "In an armed madhouse… where you accuse your doctors of insanity and plot the Hebrew socialist revolution against the fascist national Golgotha." Part III, "Howl."

*

For the last ten weeks, I've been suffering from the most serious bout of insomnia I've ever experienced. I sleep an hour and a half, then I'm up, fighting with my foe, insomnia, for hours, losing, fearful of the consequences of the sun coming up on a new day of work and other responsibilities, my having slept for only ninety minutes.

Throughout the day, I feel withdrawn, isolated in the fog of exhaustion, my mind slow, my heart unable to respond to beauty, kindness, love.

As part of my daily meditation practice, I often read a few prayers, including the psalm for the day, from the traditional Jewish morning liturgy. Sometimes there's a phrase that calls out to me, and I choose to repeat it internally for the duration of my meditation practice, or I repeat it a few times at the beginning to set an intention, a direction for my morning meditation, returning to it now and then when I find myself lost in thought or fear.

Psalm 23 is not among the texts I regularly read. Let me be honest: I say regularly, but during this period of sleep deprivation, I have not been able to bring myself to read any prayers: they all feel so distant from me, so alien to me, that even reading a few words of them brings little but more pain.

One night, desperate for something to quiet my mind (worrying about work, my responsibilities as new Department Chair), I recalled a verse from Psalm 23, *He makes me lie down by still waters.* The waters of *menuchot*, deep rest, the kind of rest experienced by God on the seventh day and available to Jews who observe the Sabbath. Well, I mis-recalled that verse, but saying it and visualizing the experience of lying by the waters of *menuchot* brought me a moment of relief that night. Not sleep, but a brief cease fire in my war with insomnia.

The next morning, I reached for Robert Alter's translation of *The Book of Psalms.*

Other than one line, "Though I walk in the vale of death's shadow," which seemed and still seems strange to me (in his helpful commentary, Alter explains that his translation is an attempt to render the line in English closer to its original Hebrew), the language seemed so direct, so clear, so immediate, so fresh, so alive, so contemporary, so useful, so near:
"Though I walk in the vale of death's shadow,
   I fear no harm,
      for You are with me."
"I fear no harm/for You are with me."

As helpless, withdrawn, isolated, and utterly alone as my insomnia made me feel, these two lines comforted me. They became my go-to lines in moments of desperation: desperation for sleep, desperation to feel alive during my waking hours.

You *are* with me.

*

We know what happens before Ginsberg reassures his dear friend Carl Solomon that despite physical circumstances that would suggest otherwise, they are together. In Part I of "Howl," Ginsberg famously recounts the nightmarish, outlandish experiences of his countercultural, outcast generation—a generation of "angelheaded hipsters burning for" an "ancient heavenly connection," who in their quest follow intuition and impulse and signs: the "cosmos instinctively vibrated at their feet in Kansas."

In Part II, Ginsberg names the source of the Beat Generation's suffering:

Tiferet

Moloch, that "sphinx of cement and aluminum" that "bashed open their skulls and ate up their brains and imagination."

Then, in Part III, Ginsberg turns to address, console, assure his beloved, locked away for treatment of his "madness."

We don't know the narrative context out of which Psalm 23 emerges. But from the psalm itself, we know this: it begins (verses 1 - 3) and ends (verses 6 and 7) in the third person, the psalmist speaking *of* his Lord: "The Lord is my shepherd;" "He makes me;" "He brings;" "He leads."

Then, in the middle, in the heart of the psalm, He speaks directly to God: "You are with me." It is as if, suddenly, without warning, the psalmist has become aware of God's presence in his life. It's a fleeting but crucial moment in the psalm, in the psalmist's consciousness.

From speaking *of,* to speaking *to* without any explicit change in setting or circumstance.

The psalm brings what is distant near.

The psalm enacts a process. The process begins with the psalmist recalling past experiences of God's comfort and protection, which may be a way the psalmist reminds himself that it's possible he'll experience the same again some day. Then, there He is, potently, powerfully, graciously present, consoling, setting a table—in the presence of foes no less—and moistening the psalmist's head with oil and filling his cup to overflowing. A luxurious moment. Then, just as suddenly as God's presence appears, it disappears, but the psalmist's confidence in God's everlasting presence, even when the psalmist may not be aware of it, is reaffirmed: "I shall dwell in the House of the Lord/ for many long days."

*

You are with me, I am with you. We breathe the same air, even when we are distant from one another; say, a bowshot away.

*

That's how far apart they sat, Hagar and her child, Ishmael.

Sarah, after the birth of her own son, Isaac, didn't like what she saw, the son of Hagar the Egypt playing. The son Hagar bore with Abraham. So she ordered Abraham to send Hagar and that boy away, lest he share in Isaac's inheritance. Abraham gave them some bread and a skin of water, and sent them away.

When the water was gone, Hagar could not bear to witness her child's death of thirst. So she left him under a bush and walked away, a bowshot's distance.

Terribly alone and apart, she is overcome by the lyric impulse: she bursts into tears (cries out) or, as contemporary American Jewish songwriter, performer, and poet Alicia Jo Rabins' "Arrow and Bow" has it, into song: "I'll be over here and you stay over there/ as long as we both breathe this unforgiving air."

No angel in that air. No God. Suspend the story at that moment, feel your way into it, and you may discover the urgent need to hear someone, some being declare:

> *I am with you* (Ginsberg)
>
> You are with me
>
> *my little grain of rice, my little blueberry*
>
> *my fig, my pear, my orange--how you grew in me* (Rabins)
>
> In the face of my foes
>
> *you bang on the catatonic piano the soul is innocent and immortal it should*
>
> *never die ungodly in an armed madhouse* (Ginsberg)
>
> In the face of my foes
>
> *There are twenty-five-thousand comrades all together singing* (Ginsberg)
>
> You moisten my head with oil
>
> *I am with you in Rockland*
>
> *we both breathe this unforgiving air* (Rabins)

*

But the story doesn't end there. God hears the cry of Hagar's boy. And an angel of God calls to Hagar from heaven: "What troubles you, Hagar? Fear not, for God has heeded the cry of the boy where he is" (GEN 21: 17).

Where he is

My cup overflows

I am with you in Rockland

In the vale of death's shadow

In Rockland

I fear no harm *in Rockland*

For You are with me *I am with you*

That's the story. The song. The poem. The psalm.

Tiferet

Works Cited

The Book of Psalms: A Translation with Commentary. Translated by Robert Alter, W. W. Norton and Company, 2009.

Ginsberg, Allen. "Howl." *Collected Poems: 1947 - 1980.* Harper & Row, Publishers, 1984.

Girls in Trouble. "Arrow & Bow." *Open the Ground*, Girls in Trouble, 2015, http://www.girlsintroublemusic.com/albums/open-the-ground/

23

A David psalm.

The Lord is my shepherd,
    I shall not want.
In grass meadows He makes me lie down,
    by quiet waters guides me.
My life He brings back.
    He leads me on pathways of justice
        for His name's sake.

Though I walk in the vale of death's shadow,
    I fear no harm,
        for You are with me.
Your rod and Your staff--
    it is they that console me.
You set out a table before me
    in the face of my foes.
You moisten my head with oil,
    my cup overflows.

Let but goodness and kindness pursue me
    all the days of my life.
I shall dwell in the house of the Lord
    for many long days.

from *The Book of Psalms: A Translation and Commentary*, Robert Alter

FICTION

Meditations on Dear Petrov

Set in 19th Century Russia during a time of war

Susan Tepper

Russia

Mouth of the eastern cave leads to a tunnel I have never seen. The gypsy with the one crossed eye often speaks of it. Long. Rugged, she says. A tunnel to be reckoned with. Not for the weak says the gypsy. Her eye glints. On market day. In the tavern. Though never during winter. The gypsy must spend her winters as I do. Hidden away. All winter this house my cave. Egg walls stained. Dried out. Peeling. Reaching as if to pull away. From what. You laugh at my utterings, dear Petrov. Insisting that behind these walls lies a palace. My shoulders hunch. I can feel its deliberate pull. What could it want of me. I have nothing leftover. No crumb or potato to spare. Scarcely enough tea. I have dropped two stones in one year's time. You press me into the straw mattress. Remarking that I am a frail bird. You enter me the way you go to battle. With deliberation. How this frail bird longs to nest. Somewhere in the warmer climes. Far beyond this barren place. O Russia. Mother Land. My plan was not to desert you.

Common

Martyrs have been sacrificed in the great paintings. Room after room framed glittering gold. Splashes of red and worried skies. The gleaming blade, dear Petrov. While crows poised in trees. Mourners knelt on the ground in prayer. I saw these pictures as a child. Gripping my father's hand. In the city where the church spires shine golden too. With or without the sun. Our hands gloved and a carriage with a top and sides. Black and shiny. Robes to cover our laps. So unlike my open trap to which I tether my horse. Beloved creature. I am happy to share my potatoes. Your tongue rolls rough against my palm. After feeding I take to your flanks once more.

Tiferet

Riding slowly through this house. A clip clop. Each room the sea changing color. Green to blue to dullest gray. Deplorable ruin. Down to the cellars rough beams hanging low. You know to duck your sweeping head. This trick I have learnt from you. My friend of a thousand seasons. One common potato. Clutching your mane I promise you one more.

Grace

You instruct me to go to the church. Defy the innocents. Rub holy water on my breasts. Put my lips to the lips of God. I stand before you staring at your mouth. Unable to utter a word in reply. This journey, dear Petrov. You. Neither will be my saving grace. Salvation coming from the rocks and streams. The white birch forest. The mountain always in view. Protective. Its great size shadows the house and what I most fear. Over its top are the guns. I try to accept that sound to no avail. Will I outlive the guns and cannon fire. A soldier, you have no answer. A soldier coated in the stench of war. Though I brushed your coat and scrubbed your boots 'til my hands ached. My sink is a font. I bow to what my sink must endure. The birds come back each spring with a troubling regularity. They have the freedom to choose while I do not. I have very few freedoms. Which hat to wear. Whether to darn my cloak or go ragged. The saints went ragged I say. Causing you to laugh considerably. Loud and bellowing. Crashing. Knocking your whisky over. I cover my ears and move toward the kitchen looking out its one smudged window. Singing a soft muted prayer. *O black birds of Russia I know it isn't true, the fire still burns bright in you.*

FICTION

The Spiral

Katherine L. Weaver

"Where are we?" my mom asks. She is in foreign territory. The mountains that lace the highway make her nervous. The long desert stretches alarm her. A Midwesterner, she cannot orient herself. "What if we break down? Who will find us?"

"My car is sturdy. We're not going to breakdown. It'll be okay," I say.

"Where are we going?" she asks.

"Carson City," I say.

"What's there?"

"A pow-wow. Ever been to one?"

"No." She clips off the word. Her mouth purses. She stares out the window, disappointed.

My mother is a sixty-five-year-old mother of seven, widowed for twenty-five years. She has flown with my sister, Tammy, from Missouri to Nevada and is excited and unsure. She has read all of the murder mysteries of Cady Jane Roberts and her cats. This is her first visit out West since she lived here thirty years ago. It will be the last and final vacation of her life. She has mellowed over the years, her anger no longer sharp and critical. But I sense it lies dormant, just at the raw edges of her, waiting to be called forth.

"What interest would that hold for me?" she asks using her formal, distant voice that means she's too good to go to Carson City.

"Well, we are Cherokee, Mom," I say. I see the veins in her neck stand out a little as she grimaces. "You alright?"

"Yes, I'm fine." I notice she holds her right hand tightly over her mouth and looks out over the sage-brushed desert floor. Missouri stoicism.

"Okay," I say. I am 12 years old again, defending myself.

How can I explain? How can I explain that I want to share my love for this land with her? My love for the Natives and for my Native self? How can I awaken in her the beauty of our Cherokee heritage? Of our Ancestors? Of the Grandfathers?

I park the car and we walk out onto a dirt-packed road. Drums vibrate the ground and songs echo in all directions. To the left, a yellow-topped sagebrush blooms. Time to gather the white sage.

The dust and wind makes Mom and Tammy sneeze.

"We are allergic to sagebrush," Mom says.

"Nonsense," I say. "We're Indians. Indians can't be allergic to sagebrush."

Mom frowns.

Tammy stops sneezing and smiles at me.

We walk past a remnant of the Carson Indian Boarding School. I shiver a little. The school sits off to one side, constructed of rough red, black and white stone walls and a slanted, sagging roof. The windows are boarded up. The stairs crumbling. A shadowed reminder of the past.

"What's that?" asks Mom.

"The old Indian boarding school."

"Ye gods, it looks grim," she says.

"Yeah, it was – children forcibly taken from their homes, beaten, converted…"

"Converted?" she asks.

"Converted into Christians," I say.

"Hell's bells. You must be kidding. The sons of bitches."

Mom is an agnostic. Forced to go to church as a child, she swore that none of her children would ever see the inside of one. She kept true to her oath despite my father's few unsuccessful attempts to take us.

She stops for a moment and places her hands on one of the broken-down walls. "Damn. I can almost hear the little children crying for home."

I am surprised at this. Her empathy is something new to me.

Softly, I say, "Yeah."

"I know just how they feel," she says.

I see the kindness in her now. I have only seen this expression on her face once. Long ago in a photo when she was a young mother, holding me in her arms.

The drums reverberate like a heartbeat from the pow-wow grounds, calling to us.

Mom removes her hand from the wall and walks toward the sound. "Let's go," she says.

We walk to the arena built on flat land, scraped clear of sage and sand and prepared with fresh earth. Sheltering green trees of cottonwood and juniper surround it. The earth smells new and alive here.

White canvas tents mushroom around the area, shading Native vendors who sell their wares on folding tables: books, beaded jewelry and leather-tooled art. The tables buzz with activity and low-priced deals.

An old double-wide trailer bears a sign: "Two Indian tacos and a soft drink – $2.50." Several middle-aged Native women work inside, smiling and visiting. The smell of bubbling oil permeates the air as they drop raw frybread dough into the deep, hot vat.

Four Paiute men sit around a large, round drum, pounding out the song's rhythms with traditional drumsticks of rawhide and feathers. One of them sings in a high-pitched voice, leading the others who chant in lower tones. Their words are punctuated with shouts and cries.

My feet dance all by themselves as the music moves them.

My sister and mother follow me, smiling self-consciously.

We step our way through the closely packed crowd: tourists wearing beaded bolos, costumed dancers, tall-hatted cowboys.

A Shoshone woman walks by, holding her two-year-old asleep in her arms.

"Poor little guy. He's all worn out," Mom says.

Wistful, Mom smiles at me.

I need to find a place for her to sit.

A seven-year-old boy rushes by and stares at Mom.

Tentative, she says, "Hi."

He stops, drinks his soda and glares.

"Come on, Mom." I guide her through the crowd.

"Why did he look at me like that?' she asks.

"He doesn't know you. In his world, eye contact is reserved for friends or family. You are a stranger to him."

"Well, I'd be his friend," she says.

I've never known Mom to be so sensitive. "It's not personal, Mom. Don't take it that way."

"It's personal to me," she says.

Remarkably, her feelings are hurt. "Mom, let's go," I say.

Mom laces her hands over her waist and walks, head down.

She looks up as a sweet-faced baby gurgles from a cradleboard, carried by her mother.

"She smiled at me," Mom whispers.

"Yes, she did," says the round-faced Paiute woman.

Mom beams a smile at baby and mother. They laugh.

Mother and child walk on.

"See. They didn't know me either. But they were friendly."

"Okay." I smile.

Tiferet

I hold Mom's hand. It's warm and dry. We walk through the crowd as Tammy follows. "Let's find a seat," I say.

Tammy is a thirty-two-year-old slender, petite woman. She has lived with Mom all her life since her childhood accident. Ten months after our father died, Tammy fell down a flight of stairs in the basement and landed on her head, which caused her to suffer a grand-mal seizure. She was seven. She is shy and normally does not talk. As the baby of the family, she is favored by everyone.

Waves of heat rise from the metal bleachers. "There's no awning above the bleachers? I'll burn in this hot sun," Mom says.

I arrange my shawl on one of the bleachers, covering a space for her to sit. I remove my hat and place it on her head. I take a plastic water bottle from my bag and give it to her. "Here, Mom," I say.

She drinks.

"Sit here —" I pat the covered seat.

"I can't," she says. "I look ridiculous in this hat."

"No, you don't," I say. I hug her and she stiffens slightly. She is not prepared for my sudden show of affection.

Unenthused, she sits like a petulant child. She places her purse beside her. "Do you at least have some sunscreen?" she asks.

"Yes." I fish it out of my bag and hand it to her.

"Thanks," she says and slathers it on her arms, face and neck. She hands the sunscreen to Tammy, who applies it as well.

"We can leave if you want," I say.

Mom begins to collect her purse and rises when Tammy says, "No, I want to stay. I like the dancers."

Mom stops. She will do anything for Tammy. As will I. She puts her purse back down and sits. Mom sighs. The muscles in her jaw tighten. "Well, I could use an Indian taco and something sweet to drink."

"Comin' right up."

"I'm coming with you," says Tammy.

"I think you should stay with Mom. I'll be right back," I say.

Tammy looks at her feet.

"I'll be alright. You two just go along." Mom sets her jaw Missouri-style and looks away from us.

Tammy bounds away like a deer. "Hold on, Tammy."

"We'll be right back," I say to Mom.

"I'll be fine," she blurts.

I straighten her hat.

She swats my hand away.

"Right back."

Mom nods. For the first time, I see Mom as an older woman. Not the feisty, unreasonable mother of my teenage youth. She has grown time-worn and fragile over the years. There is great beauty that comes with this ripening of age and it shines on her face and hands now.

"Right back," I say again.

She waves me on.

Tammy and I walk to the old trailer and stand in a long line, watching the dancers as we wait our turn. I can see Mom from where we stand.

"She's fine," says Tammy.

"I know," I say, but I keep my eyes on Mom anyway. She looks slumped over, her hat awry.

In the arena, women of all ages appear, wearing brightly colored dresses of turquoise, red, yellow and pink. Tiny, metal cones hang in scalloped rows on their skirts and blouses, making jingling sounds as they move. The music is lively as the dancers slide to the rhythm of the beat without lifting their feet off the ground.

"These are Fancy Dancers," I say to Tammy.

"What tribe are they?" asks Tammy.

"They are Shoshone," I say.

"They're beautiful," says Tammy. "Look at that woman's moccasins." A dancer in blue wears yellow-beaded leggings over her moccasins. At the heel of each foot, a flapping bluebird flies in vibrant colors.

The music quickens and the Fancy Dancers lift their feet off the ground. First, one foot lifts and returns to the ground, then the other. The tin cones produce metallic accompaniment to the music. Some of the dancers hold the wing of an eagle above their heads. Others hold the wing close to their waists.

"The dance of the Fairy People," Tammy says.

It is so like Tammy to make this whimsical comparison. She, too, could be one of these Winged Ones.

"Tell me about the Fairy People again from long ago," she says.

I am surprised that she remembers this story from our childhood. I told her about the Fairy People when she was three. Since the accident, her early memories are scarce.

"The Fairy People are the most beautiful and graceful of all of the Ancient People. They live in the woods and beside the streams in the forests of Cherokee, North

Tiferet

Carolina. Our Ancestors used to call to them for their blessings and protection."

"Are the Fairy People myths?" asks Tammy.

"No. They are living, breathing beings who speak in poetry and fly from pure joy."

The music moves faster. The women hold up their shawls of pink, purple and white, extending both arms, displaying designs of oval, diamond and rainbow shapes embroidered upon them. The long fringes of their shawls sway and rise. The dancers swirl faster and faster. Their swift steps blur as they rise gracefully into the air with high, bouncing steps. Higher and higher they leap. Quicker and quicker they dance.

"They are flying," says Tammy.

I put my arm around her. I feel the delicate bones under her soft shoulders.

She shakes with laughter.

I glance over at Mom.

She sits quietly.

The music quickens now as men dressed in colors of blue and green enter. Their upper arms are bare except for the metal bands around them. They wear three rows of large, silver bells just under their knees. Their moccasins are white, as are the headbands tied around their foreheads.

Tammy moves closer to me. "Who are they?" she asks.

"They are the Sage Grouse Dancers," I say.

"What are they doing?" asks Tammy.

"They're dancing like the quail that live in the sagebrush. They hide and maneuver carefully in the underbrush. But when startled, they explode into flight, like you."

Tammy laughs. "Like you," she wisecracks. She crosses her arms. "I am not a grouse."

"I said a grouse, not a grouch," I tease.

The Sage Grouse Dancers wear feathered headpieces that form circles on their heads and tie under their chin. One grouse feather rises vertically from the crown of each dancer's head. The men dance. They strut and spiral in large circles. They droop their arms. They stand upright. They bend down low to the ground. They twirl, then move forward.

The Native woman calls, "Next?"

Tammy and I step to the window of the trailer. We order tacos and Cokes. I pay and we wait.

The music begins to pound, speed up. I turn around and look for Mom on the bleachers. I see her. She is not alone.

"Hurry," I say to Tammy.

We rush back, abandoning our refreshments.

"Hey," I say to Mom.

142

A slight, wizened Native woman sits beside her.

"This is Shirley Smith. She's a Paiute," Mom says. Mom is relaxed, as if she has known this woman forever.

"Very nice to meet you," I say.

Shirley smiles at me with the sweetest smile I have ever seen.

"Shirley is telling me all about the dances," says Mom.

"She is?" I say.

Shirley looks pleased.

"Do you know what the Sage Grouse Dance means?" asks Mom.

"No," I say.

"Well, the dance is all about spirals." She is excited. She speaks quickly. "See how the men dance in circles — above, below?"

"Yes."

"They are dancing the rhythm of life." Mom smiles at Shirley, nods.

Shirley nods in return, encouraging her to go on.

"It is the dance of life and death and renewal," says Mom.

I chuckle. "Very good."

Mom smiles. "The dancer carries wisdom around the spiral as he connects with the flow of life."

"Impressive," I say. "I like it."

Mom looks at Shirley.

Shirley giggles.

"But the spiral is also the storm." Ominously, Mom wrinkles her forehead. "The hurricane, the tornado, the whirlpool." She is enjoying herself. "The dance reminds us to stay calm even when the storm rages around us."

The storm rages around us echoes in my mind.

Mom says, "The spiral is the wheel of the Milky Way. It is the soul's journey through time." Her hands circle dramatically.

I love seeing her this way. The soul? I have never heard her speak of the soul.

"But be cautious," Mom says, raising one finger in the air. "If you travel to the center of the spiral, it can lift you up or undo you."

I shiver.

I have never heard my mother talk like this. Infused with the joy of the People. Comforted by the generosity of a Native woman. Inspired and alight with new discovery.

I thank Shirley in my mind.

Quietly, Shirley nods, acknowledging me.

I bow my head to her. Humble. Grateful.

Tiferet

Exhausted, we pile into the car, the music still pounding in our ears. I drive onto the dirt road. Mom does not speak.

When we reach the highway, she says, "That was nice."

"I'm glad you liked it."

Mom grows quiet, sullen.

"Mom, are you alright?"

"I'm perfectly fine." Her jaw is set.

Carefully, I say, "Are you sure?"

"Yes."

"I could pull over –"

"No." She sits rigid, grimacing in pain.

I pull over, turn off the engine and hold her hand. She is shaking.

Tammy, sitting in the backseat, pulls away.

Mom's features are irregular, distorted as if one half of her face is lifting and the other half is drooping. "I am not an Indian," she says to me.

I stroke her hand.

"I am an Indian," she says to me.

I squeeze her hand.

Her eyes cloud. She speaks only to herself now. "I am — I'm not. I am — I'm not." She is far away now. "I hate Indians. I love Indians — I hate them — I love them — I —" She begins to cry.

I hold her as her body sways from side to side, her shoulders trembling.

She is torn between her grief and her disgust for herself. Her unknowing. Her shame. Her undiscovered self. The dance. The People have brought it all up to her.

We sit awhile, holding each other.

The next day they fly home to Missouri.

They never return to Nevada.

And Mom and I never speak of it again.

The Spiral.

Shirley.

Becoming undone.

I visit my Paiute Mother on the reservation. The wood is neatly stacked in three small piles outside of her front door where I have left them. I grab a handful and knock on her door.

A diminutive, sweet, caramel-voiced woman opens the door and throws her arms around me with excitement. "Come in," she says.

I kiss her on the cheek.

She smiles. "I'll get some coffee," she says.

I walk to the stove, open the round, metal top with its handle. I place the wood into the stove. I stir it until it settles and the fire catches evenly. I place the top back onto the stove. I sit.

"It's still hot," she says.

She brings me coffee in a blue, chipped enamel cup. We sit drinking it and looking out the window. We sit in silence, savoring the coffee, basking in the warmth of the stove's fire. And in each other's company.

A tree grows outside, larger than I remember. It still holds autumn leaves, brightly colored in reds and yellows. The wind blows, dancing the leaves.

How did the tree grow so quickly without me noticing? As if its growth were invisible?

"Coffee's good," I say.

"Thank you," she says, her head bends slightly.

Then I know.

I am this autumn tree refashioned by my Paiute Spiritual Mother sitting beside me, grown in deep-rooted, reliable earth.

I am home.

A Review of

The Best Lover

BY EDWIN ROMOND

THE BEST LOVER
By Laura Boss
NYQ Books
75 Pages
$15.95 Paperback

ISBN: 978-1-63045-044-1
To order: https://www.amazon.com/Best-Lover-Laura-Boss/dp/1630450448/ref=sr_1_1?ie=UTF8&qid=15 34523067&sr=8-1&keywords=the+best+lover+laura +boss

When I arrived at the last page of *The Best Lover*, Laura Boss' wonderful new collection, I found myself thinking of the song, "Seasons of Love" from *Rent* that asks, "How do you measure a life of a woman or a man?" In poems that are often hilarious, sometimes heartbreaking, but always supremely crafted, Boss measures her life in verse that shows both the beauty and power of putting oneself on paper.

Laura Boss' blunt honesty begins with the title poem, "The Best Lover,"

I tell every man I'm with
  that he's the best lover
  I've ever had

He always believes me.

A few poems later in "What I Don't Believe," Boss continues that candor with a funny/sad accounting of a J-Date experience:

On the first J-Date at coffee
  "How much do you weigh?"
  my date asks me
  How much money do you have?
  he asks.

Throughout *The Best Lover* Boss dazzles with language. In "Snapshot," she somberly describes World War II soldiers who are

> *soon to ship out to Europe —*
> *out to Pacific waters*
> *on a bon voyage blood and death journey.*

Sometimes Boss touches a variety of bases between the first and final lines. In "Ode to My GPS," for example, she introduces us to her Aunt Henrietta who

> *did not hesitate to tell you*
>   *when you were wrong.*

and follows that with a comical narration of getting lost after giving a poetry reading and. While we're still smiling, she concludes the poem with this touching declaration:

> *And like my GPS, Aunt Henrietta never*
> *had affection in her voice*
> *though you knew when you were with her*
> *you could always count on her*
> *to help you find your way home.*

I admire how Laura Boss consistently confirms William Carlos Williams' dictum that "anything is grist for a poem." In "Birdbaths," she starts with the sight of hungry and busy birds where the bluebirds seemed "like happy bullies" among the wrens, robins, and cardinals, then changes focus to a description of her grandmother, who never remembered:

> *the exact amounts of flour, butter,*
> *or walnuts for her brittle Mandel Bread*
> *though I always thought I'd never tasted*
> *anything so sumptuous ...*

Tiferet

That memory, warm and inviting, leads Boss to conclude the poem with an even deeper discovery that her grandmother's inclination to not remember exactly the baking ingredients is

perhaps not so different from every
spontaneous measure of love we receive —
never exact or precise but
somehow still just right.

Several poems deal powerfully with Boss's Jewish heritage and growing up and living among non-Jewish people. A deeply painful moment in this book occurs in Boss' poem, "Fourth Grade" when:

a boy I thought liked me
called me a "dirty Jew"
as I was walking home after school
My face blazed like a ripe tomato
I didn't say anything back to him
but ran the rest of the way home crying.

In "Singing Christmas Carols…" Boss writes of being "one of the only Jewish kids" in public school during the Christmas season:

when my classmates and I gathered the day before Christmas break
in the school auditorium of Public School — Number 11 to sing
Christmas carols …

And though I loved the music of "Silent Night, "Joy to the World,"
" Come All Ye Faithful"
still every time the words "Baby Jesus" or "Christ" came up
I would open my mouth into an "O" but never say those words
somehow thinking I was not betraying my religion,
somehow staying Jewish despite the seduction of the music.

Boss goes on to give a ringing affirmation of her heritage In "Your Face is the Map of Israel," when a London cab driver asks, "Are you from Israel?" and Boss responds:

"No, I'm Jewish but none of my family is from Israel —
I'm from New Jersey," I say
I decide to take his remark as a compliment.

One of the book's longest and strongest selections is "9/11." This is surely a subject many poets have written about, but Boss makes it personal and, in doing so, makes its pathos universal. Boss chooses to narrate the poem in present tense, a decision that intensifies the story of the poem and makes the reader feel as if she is living each horrifying second with her:

My old college roommate calls — the phones are back —She's crying
"Where were you? Are you alright?'
My older son calls from Washington to tell me he and his wife (who
works for the federal government) are OK and checking to make
sure I'm fine.

As familiar as the tragedy of 9/11 is, Boss illuminates the sadness even further by vividly describing its impact upon her granddaughter:

It will be two more days before the principal of my six-year-old
granddaughter's school will call to say Amanda Rose's
first grade desk mate's father is "missing."

One of the most poignant lines appears near the poem's conclusion when Boss describes the nighttime view of Manhattan from her window:

Through my window I see the Empire State Building is dark
where usually it's ablaze each night ...

But tonight it is dark (something I don't ever remember seeing)
It is as if the now tallest building in the City is in mourning for
New York ...

Laura Boss' *The Best Lover* is a wise and insightful volume written with both charm and authority. In poem after poem, Boss leads us on a journey across the landscape of her life, and, in the process, lets us find ourselves along the way.

Contributors

GAYLE BRANDEIS (EDITOR-IN-CHIEF)

Gayle is the author of *Fruitflesh: Seeds of Inspiration for Women Who Write* (HarperOne), *Dictionary Poems* (Pudding House Publications), and the novels *The Book of Dead Birds* (HarperCollins), which won Barbara Kingsolver's Bellwether Prize for Fiction of Social Engagement, *Self Storage* (Ballantine), *Delta Girls* (Ballantine), and *My Life with the Lincolns* (Henry Holt Books for Young Readers), which received a Silver Nautilus Book Award and was chosen as a state-wide read in Wisconsin. Two books are forthcoming in 2017, a memoir, *The Art of Misdiagnosis: Surviving My Mother's Suicide* (Beacon Press) and a collection of poetry, *The Selfless Bliss of the Body* (Finishing Line Press). Her work has appeared in such publications as Salon, The Rumpus, The Nation, and The San Francisco Chronicle; one of her essays was listed as "Notable" in Best American Essays 2016. She was named a Writer Who Makes a Difference by The Writer Magazine. She served as Inlandia Literary Laureate from 2012-2014 and currently teaches at Sierra Nevada College and the low residency MFA program at Antioch University, Los Angeles.

PHYLLIS BARBER

Phyllis Barber has published eight books--a novel, two books of short stories, a trilogy of memoir, and two books for children, and won the Associated Writing Programs Award in Creative Nonfiction for *How I Got Cultured: A Nevada Memoir*. In her creative world, she shadow boxes with a grand piano, fiction, and creative non-fiction, and is currently revising a new novel, *Adababa and the Third Wife*.

MARCIA KRAUSE BILYK

Marcia Krause Bilyk is a retired UM pastor, who after breaking her femur in a moped accident, realized it was time to do the things she'd always wanted to do, like take a photography course. She's attended photo workshops in Maine, NYC, Hungary, and the Czech Republic. She lives in rural NJ with her husband and three dogs.

JONATHAN BLUNK

Jonathan Blunk is a poet, critic, essayist, and radio producer. His work has appeared in *The Nation, Poets & Writers, The Green Mountains Review* and elsewhere. He was a co-editor of *A Wild Perfection*, the selected letters of James Wright.

LAURA BOSS

Laura Boss is a first place winner of the Poetry Society of America's Gordon Barber Poetry Contest. She was the sole representative of the USA at the XXVI International Struga Poetry Festival. In 2011 she received the First International Poetry Prize at the First International Poetry Festival in Swansea, Wales. She is a recipient of three NJSCA Poetry Fellowships. Founder and Editor of the poetry magazine *Lips,* her own most recent books include *Arms: New and Selected Poems* and *Flashlight* (both Guernica Editions). A Dodge Poet, her poems have appeared in *The Poets of New Jersey from Colonial to Contemporary* and *The New York Times.*

JOHN BRANTINGHAM

John Brantingham is Sequoia and Kings Canyon National Park's first poet laureate. His work has been featured in hundreds of magazines and *The Best Small Fictions 2016.* He has ten books of poetry and fiction including *The L.A. Fiction Anthology* (Red Hen Press) and *A Sublime and Tragic Dance* (Cholla Needles Press). He teaches at Mt. San Antonio College.

CINDY CARLSON

When not traveling and birding with her husband, Cindy has spent most of her adult life along Virginia's Chesapeake Bay. After a long career in youth development, she is enjoying retirement as a writer. A winner of the Hampton Roads Writers contest for creative nonfiction and a reader for WHRO radio's Writers Block, her work has appeared several travel journals, *The Quotable, The Wayfarer, Bird's Thumb,* and is forthcoming in *Chautauqua* and *Barely South Review.*

ADRIAN ERNESTO CEPEDA

Adrian Ernesto Cepeda is the author of the poetry collection *Flashbacks & Verses… Becoming Attractions* from Unsolicited Press and the poetry chapbook *So Many Flowers, So Little Time* from Red Mare Press. Adrian is an LA Poet who has a BA from the University of Texas San Antonio and an MFA degree from Antioch University in Los Angeles where he lives with his wife and their cat Woody Gold. Connect with Adrian at: http://www.adrianernestocepeda.com.

RICHARD CHESS

Richard Chess is the author of four books of poetry, most recently *Love Nailed to the Doorpost* (University of Tampa Press 2017). His work has been included in *Best American Spiritual Writing 2005* and *The Bloomsbury Anthology of Contemporary American Jewish Poetry.* He is a regular contributor to "Good Letters," the blog hosted by Image. He directs the Center for Jewish Studies at UNC Asheville. You can find out more about him at his website: www.richardchess.com.

HEIDI CLAPP-TEMPLE

Artist Heidi Clapp-Temple stages visual narratives depicting scenes full of emotion, with a particular focus on dreams, fantasy, and memories. Her combination of various mediums with photography allows her to create a unique visual language full of symbolism, textures, and complex layers. You can view more of her work at www. HeidiClappTemple.com.

JENNIFER CLEMENTS

Jennifer Clements is an architect, transpersonal psychologist, and teacher who moved from San Francisco to an island off the coast of Maine to write fiction. Her stories have appeared in *Gettysburg Review, Witness, Maine Review*, and other journals. She also has earlier non-fiction and academic publications.

REBECCA EVANS

Rebecca Evans is a decorated Gulf War veteran and mentors teens in the juvenile system. Her work has appeared in *Gravel Literary* magazine, *Scribes Weekly, Willow Down Books*, and is forthcoming in *War, Literature & the Arts* and *Fiction Southeast*. She is pursuing her MFA in Creative Nonfiction Writing at Sierra Nevada College and serves on the editorial staff of *Sierra Nevada Review*. She lives in Idaho with her three sons.

HEDY HABRA (CONTRIBUTOR & COVER ARTIST)

Hedy Habra has authored two poetry collections, *Under Brushstrokes*, finalist for the USA Best Book Award and the International Poetry Book Award, and *Tea in Heliopolis*, winner of the USA Best Book Award and finalist for the International Poetry Book Award. Her story collection, *Flying Carpets,* won the Arab-American National Book Award's Honorable Mention and was finalist for the Eric Hoffer Award. An eight-time nominee for the Pushcart Prize and Best of the Net, her work appears in *Cimarron Review, The Bitter Oleander, Blue Fifth Review, Cider Press Review, Fifth Wednesday Journal, Drunken Boat, Gargoyle, Nimrod, Poet Lore, World Literature Today* and *Verse Daily*. Her website is hedyhabra.com.

STEPHANIE BARBÉ HAMMER

Stephanie Barbé Hammer is a 5 time Pushcart Prize nominee in fiction, nonfiction, and poetry. She has published work in a bunch of journals including *Hayden's Ferry, Birds We Piled Loosely,* and the *Goldman Review*. She is the author of *How Formal?, The Puppet Turners of Narrow Interior and Delicious Strangeness: a pocket guide to Magical Realism*. She teaches creative writing at Hugo House and the Inlandia Institute.

ROGER HOUSDEN

Roger Housden is the author of the new book *Ten Poems for Difficult Times*, the most recent addition to his best-selling *Ten Poems* series, which began in 2001 with *Ten Poems to Change Your Life*. He offers writing workshops, both live and online, with an emphasis on self-discovery and exploration. Visit him online at www. RogerHousden.com.

ANDREW HUDGINS

Andrew Hudgins is Humanities Distinguished Professor Emeritus at Ohio State. Now retired, he lives in rural Tennessee with his wife, Erin McGraw. His most recent books are *A Clown at Midnight: New Poems* (Houghton Mifflin Harcourt, 2013) and *The Joker: A Memoir* (Simon and Schuster, 2013).

ESTHER WHITMAN JOHNSON

Esther Whitman Johnson, an educator from SW Virginia, volunteers on five continents, often writing about her journeys. She has completed fifteen international builds in countries ranging from Madagascar to Mongolia. Her writing has appeared in over two dozen publications. Her writing has appeared in over two dozen journals and anthologies, most recently *Forgotten Women* and *Black Lives Have Always Mattered*.

ANDREW KAUFMAN

Andrew Kaufman's books include *Earth's Ends*, winner of the Pearl Poetry Award, the *Cinnamon Bay Sonnets*, winner of the Center for Book Arts book award, *Both Sides of the Niger* (Spuyten Duyvil Press), and the *Complete Cinnamon Bay Sonnets* (Rain Mountain Press). A recipient of an NEA award in poetry, he is currently completing a book of poems based on his encounters in Rwanda with genocide survivors and perpetrators. He lives in New York City.

ADELE KENNY

Adele Kenny, author of 24 books and founding director of the Carriage House Poetry Series, has been Tiferet's poetry editor since 2006. Among other awards, she has received poetry fellowships from the NJ State Arts Council, a Merton Poetry of the Sacred Award, and Kean University's Distinguished Alumni Award. Her book, *A Lightness, A Thirst, or Nothing at All*, was a 2016 Paterson Poetry Prize Finalist.

JULIA Y. KNOBLOCH

Julia Y. Knobloch is a former journalist turned translator, project manager, and poet.

She occasionally blogs for ReformJudaism.org and was among the recipients of a 2017 Brooklyn Poets Fellowship. Her poems are published or forthcoming with *Jewish Currents, Mo*ment *Magazine, Rascal, Green Mountains Review, Jewcy, Yes Poetry Magazine,* and elsewhere. She lives in Brooklyn.

MARIE-ELIZABETH MALI

Marie-Elizabeth Mali is the author of *Steady, My Gaze* (Tebot Bach, 2011) and coeditor with Annie Finch of the anthology, *Villanelles* (Everyman's Library Pocket Poets, 2012). Her work has appeared in *Calyx, New Ohio Review*, and *Poet Lore*, among others. She is also a life coach and underwater photographer, and can be found online at www.memali.com.

EMMA MARGRAF

Emma Margraf is former foster parent, writer, communications professional, host of the local civics podcast Oly Talks, and lover of stories. Her work has also appeared in *Manifest Station, Lunch Ticket*, and *Entropy Magazine*. She holds an MFA from Antioch University in Los Angeles.

SHARA McCALLUM

Originally from Jamaica, Shara McCallum is the author of five books of poetry, published in the US & UK. Her most recent book is *Madwoman,* winner of the 2018 OCM Bocas Prize for Poetry. She also writes personal essays, which have appeared in *Creative Nonfiction, Witness*, and elsewhere.

TOM PLANTE

Tom Plante was born in New York City. He studied Geography at the University of California, Berkeley, and worked for several newspapers, including *The Berkeley Barb, The Irish Echo*, and *The Courier News*. Tom published *Berkeley Works* magazine (1981-85) and has published the poetry journal *Exit 13 Magazine* since 1988. His recent collection of poems is *Atlas Apothecary* (Finishing Line, 2016). Tom lives in Fanwood, New Jersey, with his wife and daughter.

SUSAN ROGERS

Susan Rogers is a practitioner of Sukyo Mahikari—a spiritual practice promoting positivity. Her poetry is included in numerous anthologies and journals including, *Kyoto Journal, Tiferet, Saint Julian's Press*. Watch "The Origin is One" at https://www.youtube.com/watch?v=rzPA9zeC0Qc. She was interviewed on KPFK by Lois P. Jones and nominated for a Pushcart in 2013 and 2017.

EDWIN ROMOND

Edwin Romond's latest poetry collection is *Alone with Love Songs* (Grayson Books.) He has been awarded writing fellowships from the National Endowment for the Arts, the National Endowment for the Humanities, and from both the New Jersey and Pennsylvania State Councils on the Arts. His poems have twice been featured by Garrison Keillor on NPR, and he has read three times at the Geraldine R. Dodge Poetry Festival. Romond was the recipient of the 2013 New Jersey Poetry Prize for his poem, "Champion." A native of Woodbridge, NJ he now lives with his wife, Mary, and their son, Liam, in Wind Gap, PA.

ROBERT ROSENBLOOM

Bob Rosenbloom lives in Bound Brook with his wife. His poetry has appeared in past issues of *Edison Literary Review*, the *Paterson Literary Review, US 1 Worksheets* and *LIPS*. He shared first prize in PLR's 2017 Ginsberg Poetry Contest. His chapbook, *Reunion*, was published by Finishing Line Press, 2010.

STUART SCHAEFER

Stuart Schaefer has been a freelance photographer for over 40 years. During his tour of duty in the military, he discovered an interest in photography. He then had a successful career as a post photographer for Redstone Arsenal (Huntsville, Alabama). Stuart moved to Gulf Breeze, Florida in 1992, and since then his work has been featured in *Sailing World Magazine, Backpacker Magazine, Pensacola Visitor's Guide* and other publications.

NANCY SCOTT

Nancy Scott has been managing editor of *U.S. 1 Worksheets,* journal of the U.S.1 Poets' Cooperative in NJ, for many years. Widely published in journals and anthologies, she has authored nine poetry collections. Her decades-long career as a caseworker for the State of NJ included work in a child abuse and neglect unit, as well as with foster children, homeless families, and people with mental illness and AIDS. A Ragdale Fellowship recipient, she is also an award winning collage and acrylics artist. Website: www.nancyscott.net.

TOVLI SIMIRYAN

Tovli is an award-winning writer living in Cleveland, OH with her husband, Yosif. The family arrived in America as refugees from the former Soviet Union (Moldova) in 1992. Tovli's writings have appeared in a variety of literary magazines including: *Ariga, Chabad Magazine, Jewish Magazine, Jewish Ideals-Conversations* and *Raving Dove*. She has published two volumes of poetry: *The Breaking of the Glass* and

Fixing the Broken Glass. Tovli can be reached at: https://www.facebook.com/writingonclouds/ tovli102@outlook.com or her website: http://tovlis.wixsite.com/tovliwriter.

SUSAN TEPPER

Susan Tepper is the author of seven published books of fiction and poetry. Her latest title *Monte Carlo Days & Nights* (Rain Mountain Press, NYC) is a novella set at the French Riviera. Prior to taking up the writing life, she worked as an actress, singer, flight attendant, marketing manager, TV producer, rescue worker, interior decorator, tour guide and more. Her author/book interviews can be read at the Boston Small Press & Poetry Scene. For more please visit www.susantepper.com.

MELISSA STUDDARD

Melissa Studdard's books include the poetry collection *I Ate the Cosmos for Breakfast* and the novel *Six Weeks to Yehidah.* Her writings have appeared in a wide range of publications, such as *The Guardian, Poets & Writers, Southern Humanities Review, The New York Times, Harvard Review,* and *Psychology Today.* She is the executive producer and host of VIDA *Voices & Views* for VIDA: Women in Literary Arts and an editor for American Microreviews and Interviews.

SUSAN J. TWEIT

Susan J. Tweit is a plant biologist who studied wildfires, grizzly bear habitat and sagebrush before turning to writing. Her twelve books have won national and regional awards, and include *Walking Nature Home*, a memoir. Tweit's work has appeared in magazines and newspapers from *Audubon* and *Popular Mechanics* to *High Country News* and the *Los Angeles Times.* She is a contributor for Houzz.com, and lives in Wyoming.

EMILY VOGEL

Emily Vogel's poetry, reviews, essays, and translations have been published widely, most recently in *PEN, Omniverse,* and *The North American Review.* She is the author of five chapbooks and three full-length collections, the most recent being *Dante's Unintended Flight* (NYQ Books 2017). She has a children's book, *Clara's Song* due to be released in the Spring of 2019 (Swingin' Bridge Books). She teaches writing at SUNY Oneonta and is married to the poet, Joe Weil.

MICHELLE AUCOIN WAIT

Michelle Aucoin Wait completed her M.A. in English at Mississippi State University.

She is currently writing and teaching in Reno, Nevada where she is beginning her second year of the M.F.A. Poetry program at the University of Nevada, Reno. Her poems appear in *The Meadow and Lady/Liberty/Lit.*

KATHERINE L. WEAVER

Katherine L. Weaver is a Cherokee writer of Creative Nonfiction stories. In 2018, she earned an MFA Degree in Creative Writing from Sierra Nevada College in Incline Village. She has been published in the *Ohio Quarterly* in poetry. A Middle School Novel, *Flame in the Dark* and a short story collection, *Children of the Rez* are forthcoming in 2019. Katherine currently lives in Fallon, Nevada and has taught Creative Writing at Western Nevada College in Minden.

JOE WEIL

Joe Weil is a professor teaching graduate and undergraduate classes at Binghamton U. He is the author of several poetry collections, most recently *A Night in Duluth* (NYQ Books). He has presented both poetry and music at such venues as the New Jersey State Performing Arts Center, the Detroit Opera House, and Poets' House. He also appeared in Bill Moyers' PBS documentary "Fooling with Words."

DAVID YASUDA

David Yasuda is a third-generation Japanese farm boy from rural Idaho. His writing has appeared in *Wired, Bicycling* and the *New York Time's The Wirecutter.* He works with notable chefs and influencers to create content for Snake River Farms and is pursuing an MFA in Creative Writing at Sierra Nevada College. Dave is an avid cyclist and accomplished home cook. He once shared a Marlboro Light with Neil Young, backstage at an Eric Clapton concert.

MICHAEL T. YOUNG

Michael T. Young is the author of two previous poetry collections and two chapbooks. Winner of the Jean Pedrick Chapbook Award, the Chaffin Poetry Award, and a NJ State Arts Council poetry fellowship, his work has been published in numerous print and online journals and anthologies, and has been featured on Verse Daily. He lives in Jersey City, NJ with his wife Chandra and their children, Ariel and Malia. Website: www.michaeltyoung.com

DÉSIRÉE ZAMORANO

A frequent contributor to the LA Review of Books, Désirée Zamorano's stories and essays have appeared in *Huizache, [PANK], Catapult* and the *Kenyon Review.* Her highly acclaimed literary novel, *The Amado Women*, was listed among "5 Must-Read books for the Summer," by Remezcla, and named among "Eleven Moving Beach Reads That'll Have You Weeping in Your Piña Colada" by Bustle. For more, visit www.desireezamorano.com.

POEMS FROM THE MALAWIAN WOMEN'S POETRY WORKSHOP:

MILDRED K. BARYA (INSTRUCTOR)

Mildred K. Barya has authored three poetry books: *Give Me Room to Move My Feet* (Amalion Publishing), *The Price of Memory After the Tsunami* (Mallory International), and *Men Love Chocolates But They Don't Say* (Femrite Publications). She has also published prose or hybrids in *Per Contra, Northeast Review, Tin House, Prairie Schooner* and *Poetry Quarterly*. She teaches creative writing and literature at the University of North Carolina-Asheville and is a board member of African Writers Trust. She blogs at: http://mildredbarya.com.

LUCKIER CHIKOPA

Luckier Chikopa is the winner of the 2015 Nsalamangwe Ya Ndakatuo (Champion of Poetry) and produced a poetry album in 2015. She has worked as a radio and television actress and producer and trained over 200 poets in nine districts of the Southern region of Malawi.

XARA HLUPEKILE

Xara Hlupekile has been scribbling on paper since she was a little girl. Now a content writer by day and a poet and short story writer by night, she is casting light on a mostly dark world, one word at a time.

AGATHA MALUNDA

Agatha Malunda is a young Malawian poet based in the city of Blantyre. She began writing poetry when she was at Chichiri Secondary school at the age of 13. Currently, she is pursuing a diploma program in Journalism at the University of Malawi, The Polytechnic. During her secondary school days, she won third place in an essay competition from Scotland known as the 'Hutch Challenge'. Agatha intends to write more and have her works published very soon.

LINLY MAYENDA

Linly Mayenda was born in the outskirts of Blantyre. She is a poet and a spoken word performer. She is a member of Pen Malawi.

BEVERLEY NAMBOZO NSENGIYUNVA (INSTRUCTOR)

Beverley Nambozo Nsengiyunva is a poet, author and professional public speaker. She is the Founding Director of the Babishai Niwe Poetry Foundation, a platform that promotes African poetry through annual poetry competitions, festivals and publications. Beverley also loves to travel and to raise her four daughters.

MATILDA PHIRI

Matilda Phiri is a poet and screenwriter living in Blantyre, Malawi with dreams of Hollywood.

GRACE ATHAUYE SHARRA

Grace Athauye Sharra, hails from Ntcheu District in Malawi. She holds a Diploma in Education and teaches languages at Mitundu Secondary School in Lilongwe, Malawi. A poet and short story writer, her works have appeared in many local and international publications including *Malawi: A Place Apart, In The Familiar Stranger and Other Stories: An Anthology For Junior Secondary School, The Grafted Tree And Other Short Stories, Call It Fate and Other Stories,* and *War Drums Are Beating*. She has also published in local newspapers and magazines.

RHODA ZULU

Rhoda Zulu is Community Mobilisation Project Officer for the Story Workshop Educational Trust in Blantyre, Malawi.

CARRIAGE HOUSE POETRY WINNERS:

RAY CICETTI

Ray Cicetti is a poet, psychotherapist and Zen teacher. He is married with a son and two grandchildren. He was born in Newark, New Jersey and now lives in Mountain Lakes, New Jersey.

SUSAN ROTHBARD

Susan Rothbard's poetry has appeared in *The Cortland Review, The Literary Review, Poet Lore, the Paterson Literary Review, The National Poetry Review,* and other journals. Her work has been featured in Ted Kooser's "American Life in Poetry" and on *Verse Daily,* and she won the 2011 Finch Prize for Poetry. She earned her MFA in creative writing from Fairleigh Dickinson University and her D.Litt. from Drew University. She teaches at Livingston High School in NJ.

Tiferet

DAVID VICENTI

David Vincenti's poems have appeared in journals including *Presence – A Journal of Catholic Poetry* and *Edison Literary Review*, and anthologies including *Rabbit Ears: TV Poems*; he has been nominated for a Pushcart Prize. His first full-length collection is *A Measure of This World: Galileo's Dialog with the Universe* (2015). David lives and writes in New Jersey (@DVincentiPoet).

Amazon #1 New Release in Grief

A beautifully poetic memoir about redeeming fraught relationships through grief

"Lovely writing and startling insights into father-daughter bonds, identity, mortality, and the vagaries of love. A compelling memoir."

—**Christina Baker Kline**, #1 *New York Times* bestselling author of *Orphan Train*

"A writer with exquisite restraint and precision. A beautiful, honest, sometimes troubling, spiritually adventurous book."

—**Richard Hoffman**, author of *Half the House* and *Love & Fury*

On Sale May 1, 2018

Now available for pre-order.
For more information, visit lisaromeo.net.

The Silver Baron's Wife

by Donna Baier Stein

"Through Stein's artistry, Baby Doe's story makes the heart ache."
- Judy Nolte Temple, Author, *Baby Doe Tabor: The Madwoman in the Cabin*

"Explosive, gripping and romantic."
- Talia Carner, Author, *Hotel Moscow, Jerusalem Maiden, China Doll*

"Donna Baier Stein paints a heartfelt, poignant picture filled with loving details of Baby Doe's celebrated life."
- Ann Parker, Author, *The Silver Rush Mystery Series*

"Donna Baier Stein writes with the grace and precision of a poet."
- Elizabeth Berg, *New York* Times best-selling Author

The Silver Baron's Wife traces the rags-to-riches-to-rags life of Colorado's Baby Doe Tabor (Lizzie). Hers is the tale of a fiercely independent woman who bucked all social expectations by working where 19th century women didn't work, becoming the key figure in one of the West's most scandalous love triangles, and, after a devastating stock market crash destroyed Tabor's vast fortune, living in eccentric isolation at the Matchless Mine.
www.donnabaierstein.com
Available on amazon.com and barnesandnoble.com

#1 New Release - Bestseller Biographical Fiction on Amazon

FOSTERING PEACE THROUGH LITERATURE & ART

30614635R00089

Made in the USA
Columbia, SC
29 October 2018